Mom for a million?

"I don't get it," Kim said. "If you needed an heir, I'm sure you could have had your pick of ladies. And why on earth would I have married *you?*"

She disregarded the obvious explanation, that this was the best-looking man a woman was ever likely to come across, and that every time his eyes searched hers, she felt as if he were touching the most intimate parts of her body.

"Do you want the real answer?" asked Prince Jacques. "Or something romantic?"

"I'm not a romantic type of person." Even with amnesia, Kim knew that to be true. "Just give it to me straight, buster."

He laughed. "All right, Princess Kimberly. And I'm well aware that you're not romantic. You didn't marry me for my title, or my irresistible charm, either. You did it for a million dollars."

"Excuse me?"

"I offered you a million dollars," he said. "And for that amount, you agreed to marry me, have my baby and then send us both back to my country while you got a divorce."

ABOUT THE AUTHOR

Jacqueline Diamond can't ski, can't dive, can barely swim, and has never been romanced by a prince, but she does have an active imagination. She also has two school-age sons and a husband with whom she has lived happily ever after for eighteen years.

Books by Jacqueline Diamond

HARLEQUIN AMERICAN ROMANCE

Jacqueline Diamond

MILLION-DOLLAR MOMMY

Harlequin Books

TORONTO • NEW YORK • LONDON
AMSTERDAM • PARIS • SYDNEY • HAMBURG
STOCKHOLM • ATHENS • TOKYO • MILAN
MADRID • WARSAW • BUDAPEST • AUCKLAND

Special thanks to Charles Lutin, M.D.

ISBN 0-373-16674-5

MILLION-DOLLAR MOMMY

Copyright © 1997 by Jackie Hyman.

Printed in U.S.A.

Chapter One

The man was gorgeous, but she didn't have a clue who he might be.

He leaned over the bed, assessing her with shadowed emerald eyes. Staring into their depths, she felt herself swept into a landscape of trackless green forests, towering mountains and misty hidden coves.

"Kim?" he said. "Can you understand me?"

"Y-yes." Her lips felt stiff, as if they belonged to someone else.

She wondered who Kim was. The man seemed to be addressing her, but her name was...her name was...

She didn't know.

If she wasn't Kim, who was she? And if she *was* Kim, why did it sound so unfamiliar?

It might help if she recognized this intense man, with his aristocratic cheekbones, sculpted light brown hair and her name on his lips. But he might as well have been a stranger.

She turned her head on the pillow. Huge vases of flowers overflowed the bedside table. She registered the fact that such lush arrangements must be expensive and wondered if she was rich, but she felt no connection to money or anything else.

Daylight slanted through venetian blinds, barring the peach-colored walls and the linoleum floor. Close by, a plastic bag hung from a metal pole, feeding liquid down a tube and into her arm. The arm sported a purplish bruise and a small scrape mark.

Wiggling her limbs, she found that they all worked, albeit somewhat painfully. A weight on her forehead might have been a bandage.

"How do you feel?" The man had a slight continental accent. "Your head must hurt."

After a moment's consideration, she identified a throbbing in her temples. "I guess it does."

"The nurse can give you pain medication, but first we have to talk." He stretched, uncramping long legs. "You need to remember what happened."

"When?" she asked.

"When you had this—accident."

She tried to concentrate on his words, but her thoughts kept straying to the man himself. There was a sharp, observant quality about him, as if he had come from a foreign land and was trying to get his bearings.

Even a woman who didn't recall her own name could see that his jacket was woven of fine material, probably part cashmere, and that it covered a handknit ski sweater of exquisite design. *He comes from a cold climate. And he's not exactly short of money.*

What was that insignia on his lapel? In the center of a rectangular green pin loomed a wolf's head with yellow eyes. In the upper left corner lay a red cross emblazoned on a white square.

It appeared to be a flag, one she had never seen

before. Or at least, she didn't think she had. It certainly wasn't *her* flag. Whatever else she might have forgotten, she could picture Old Glory with its stars and stripes.

"Kim?" said the man. "Can you tell me what happened? It's very important."

She must be Kim, since he kept calling her that. But as for how she'd landed in a hospital, the facts remained lost in the foggy recesses of her mind.

"I don't know," she said. "Uh, who are you?"

He didn't appear surprised by the question. Vaguely, Kim registered that he ought to, since he obviously knew her well enough to be ensconced in the hospital room, waiting for her to wake up.

"I'm your husband," he said, studying her reaction. "Jack."

Kim inhaled his scent, slightly piney with a hint of musk. Shouldn't she recognize the smell? "We're married?"

He produced a document from inside his jacket. Despite slightly blurry vision, she made out the names Kim Norris and Jacques LeGrand.

Since her husband had brought their marriage license to the hospital, she supposed they must be newlyweds. But he didn't act like one. He hadn't so much as smoothed back a lock of her hair or taken her hand.

Yet he watched her with a bemused expression that might indicate affection. Perhaps he was simply reserved.

Utter weariness clouded her thoughts. The last thing she noticed before she fell asleep was the wolf on his lapel. It seemed, in her blurry vision, to be watching her.

WHEN SHE WOKE AGAIN, night had fallen. The flat glare of artificial lights seemed cold, and Kim wished she could sink back into sleep.

This time, the room was full. People sat on the empty bed and on assorted chairs, talking to each other in low tones.

Were they friends or relatives? She had the sense that she ought to know them, but she didn't.

Jack stood near the door, talking to a hawklike older man in a three-piece suit. They conversed in a foreign language, possibly German, but she caught a few words that sounded French.

"She's awake!" A middle-aged woman with a warm smile leaned from the chair where Jack had sat earlier. This woman had the same emerald-green eyes, and Kim wondered if she might be her new mother-in-law. But there was an excitement in the woman's face that implied some closer relationship.

"I can't... I don't recognize... I think I have... What's the word?"

Another woman stepped forward. She was thinner and taller, with gray eyes and brown hair drawn into a French twist. "Is that a joke, Kim? You've forgotten the word *amnesia?*"

"No, Valerie, she's serious," said a masculine voice from the other side of the bed. Rolling her head, Kim took in a gray-haired man whose kind face was marred by worry lines. "The doctor warned she might have some memory lapse. She hit her head pretty hard."

"How did I—hit my head?" she asked.

"Nobody knows, exactly." The woman beside her patted Kim's hand. "You excused yourself to go to the ladies' room and the next thing we knew you were lying in the street in front of the hotel, hit by a car. The driver said you'd run out as if someone were chasing you.''

"Your wedding dress is ruined," said the thinner woman. "Now you'll never be able to tie-dye it for Halloween the way you planned." She gave a conspiratorial wink.

It seemed like an odd joke to Kim. "My wedding dress?" Apparently she'd been hit by a car on her wedding day. But why had she run into the street?

"*Was* someone chasing you?" Noiselessly, Jack had come to stand at the foot of the bed.

"I don't know." She felt an urge to cling to this man, despite his formal way of holding himself. At least she'd met him once before and knew who he was. "Does it really matter?"

Jack moved closer. "It's my responsibility to protect you, Kim."

"The doctor said she might never be able to reconstruct the moments right before the trauma," said the older man. "But the rest should come back. Honey, don't you recognize your own family?"

The whole roomful of people leaned forward expectantly. In addition to those she'd already noted, there was a young couple sitting on the spare bed and an older man, white haired and dapper, perched on a chair in the corner.

"I—I don't know any of you," Kim admitted. "Except Jack. He was here earlier."

The woman beside her flinched, and in a flash of intuition she knew this must be her mother. But why did her own parent have eyes the same unusual shade of green as Jack's?

"Mom?" she said.

Relief washed across the woman's face. "You do know me!"

Kim shook her head, and noticed that it no longer throbbed as it had in the afternoon. "I was guessing." To the man on the other side, she said, "Dad?"

He favored her with an encouraging smile. "And that's your aunt Valerie next to your mother. Valerie was your maid of honor."

The other visitors identified themselves in turn. The young couple on the other bed were her brother, Tim, and his wife, Ellen. The hawklike man in the doorway gave his name as Hans Frick, and said something about being a minister. Perhaps he had performed the ceremony.

"Don't mind me." The white-haired fellow in the corner gave a self-deprecating wave. "I'm Siegfried Merkle, the valet."

If the valet was in her hospital room, who was parking the cars? He must be off duty, but that still didn't explain his presence.

"And, uh, who am I?" she asked.

"You really have no idea?" asked her mother. "Can you remember anything?"

Kim closed her eyes and allowed her thoughts to float. "I can see a beach curving along the ocean. Above it are cliffs. There are some white buildings and a lot of pink flowers."

"That's where you live," Valerie said. "Laguna Beach." Then she added, "California. That's where we are."

Kim sank back wearily. "I'm sorry. I'm not getting anything else."

"We must have the doctor examine her before she

goes to sleep," said Jack. "She has to recover her memory."

"The neurologist makes his rounds in the morning," Valerie murmured. "I doubt there's anyone available at this hour."

"Well, someone can bloody well make himself available!" Jack gestured irritably at the valet. "Siggy, see what you can scare up, would you?"

"We appreciate your concern," said Kim's father. "But there doesn't seem to be any emergency at this point."

Jack regarded him with hooded eyes. "Not from a medical standpoint. But until we know how she came to run in front of that car, there's always the chance it will happen again, isn't there?"

The other people in the room regarded him with varying degrees of puzzlement, except for the minister, who nodded agreement.

What on earth was going on? Kim couldn't begin to figure it out. She only knew that she was growing sleepy again.

By the time a resident physician came to inform them that she could only summon the neurologist if there was some crisis, Kim was already dozing off.

THE NEXT DAY, she awakened with a ravenous appetite and a great deal more energy. The blurry vision was gone, too.

I feel more like myself, she thought, then silently acknowledged the irony of feeling like a self about whom she knew next to nothing.

She reviewed what little she had gleaned from the previous night's discussion. Apparently she felt close enough to her family to have chosen an aunt as maid of honor. And she was irreverent enough to have joked about tie-dyeing her wedding dress and wearing it for Halloween.

But what kind of work did she do? How had she met her husband? What did her home look like?

Oddly, as she listened to the bustle of orderlies delivering breakfast trays in the hallway, Kim found that she did know a number of facts.

She remembered that George Washington was the father of his country. Six plus six equaled twelve. Four quarters, ten dimes or one hundred pennies made a dollar. The Olympic games were held every four years. The best thing to do in an earthquake was to get under a heavy table or stand in a reinforced doorway.

So why couldn't she figure out how she'd come to leave her wedding reception and dash in front of a car?

The neurologist arrived at the same time as her breakfast tray. It took all of Kim's self-control to refrain from eating at once, but she managed a polite smile.

Well, at least I have good manners.

"Good morning." The doctor stopped flipping through the chart and regarded her with professional friendliness. He was dark skinned and in his forties. "How are you feeling?"

"Kind of confused," Kim admitted.

"How many fingers am I holding up?" He made a V.

"Enough to spur your team to victory."

"You're less confused than many of my colleagues," he joked. "Now let's have a look at you."

During the next few minutes, he removed her bandages and peered into her eyes. Then he asked her to walk so he could observe her balance, giving directions to turn, hop and step backward.

At the conclusion, he said, "There appears to be no serious damage. You're a very lucky young lady."

"When will I get my memory back?" she asked.

"It should return a little at a time." He made a notation in the chart. "Of course, the events right before the accident may be lost forever."

"Why?" Kim asked.

"We don't fully understand how memory works," the man said. "Our brain has a way of storing things for different periods of time, then discarding most of them. Why should you need to remember a phone number you memorized ten years ago, for example? It would only clutter up your mind."

"But this wasn't ten years ago," Kim pointed out. "I mean, was it? I haven't been in some kind of coma, have I?"

The doctor checked the chart. "No, you've been here two days. But many people, such as crime victims, block out traumatic incidents. It may be some kind of protective mechanism. In any case, we have to let nature take its course."

"When can I go home?" Kim tried to ignore the fact that she didn't know where home was.

"That depends on your progress." The neurologist's eyebrows quirked. "We don't keep people in bed as long as we used to. If you're well enough, you might go home in a day or so."

"Thank you." As the doctor left, Kim released a long breath. She couldn't help feeling that once she found herself among familiar surroundings, she would get back to normal.

Normal. But what was that? As a newlywed, she supposed she would be starting a new life.

As she tucked into her breakfast, Kim considered her impressions of her husband. She hadn't detected any loving closeness between them, but he had a natural dignity that might make him seem aloof. Surely they must have fallen in love or she wouldn't have married him.

Or perhaps, she thought glumly, her instincts about what she would and wouldn't do were all wrong. Could she have married Jack for his money? From his elegant clothes and grooming, it wasn't hard to imagine he might be wealthy.

But why would he have married her? Was she some sort of beauty? Kim glanced around the room, but there were no mirrors. She suspected her face was as black-and-blue as the bruise on her arm, but she wanted to find out as much about herself as possible.

As soon as she'd finished eating, she rang for the nurse. "I need to go to the bathroom."

The woman regarded her skeptically. "You have a catheter."

"Well, I want it out."

After checking her chart, the nurse agreed. A short time later, both the catheter and the intravenous drip had been removed. With an aide's help, Kim wobbled to the small bathroom adjoining her room. As soon as she was alone, she turned to the mirror.

The face staring back at her would have done justice to a haunted house. In addition to the large purplish bruise on her forehead, smaller cuts marked one cheek and there were dark circles under her eyes. Reddish blond hair stuck out at angles, limp from lack of washing and crumpled from the bed.

But the most startling feature was her eyes. They glowed an intense emerald green, like her mother's and like Jack's.

Kim gripped the edge of the sink to steady herself. Awakening without a memory would have been difficult enough under any circumstances, but why did it seem as if her life was a puzzle with far too many pieces missing?

She was considering pressing the red emergency buzzer for the nurse when the bathroom door swung wider. "Are you all right?" It was Jack's voice.

"Just—dizzy."

Strong hands caught her shoulders. "You shouldn't be out of bed alone."

"I wanted to see what I look like."

In the mirror, a grin slashed his face. "I hadn't pegged you as the vain type."

"It isn't vanity. I was wondering why you married me," she said.

This might have been the appropriate time for protestations of love, but none were forthcoming. Instead, Jack gave her a slight nod in the mirror. "Very well. Let's get you back to bed and I'll tell you."

A knot of apprehension clenched in Kim's chest as her husband led her out of the bathroom. What on earth was he going to say?

He guided her carefully, supporting one elbow and seeming to anticipate every wobble and hesitation. Maybe he did love her, she thought. He was certainly attuned to her.

And she to him. Despite sore muscles and a rueful awareness of her disheveled state, Kim couldn't help responding to Jack. Beneath his short-sleeved button-down shirt and crisply pressed slacks, he possessed an innate grace that was both masculine and unaffected.

It came, she assessed, from well-toned muscles and a long, lithe body. A picture flashed into her mind of joggers loping along beachfront sidewalks. "Are you a marathon runner?"

"Pardon?" He gave her a startled look.

"You're built like an athlete," she pointed out.

"I'm surprised you would notice, under the circumstances."

"I could hardly help noticing," she said.

Warmth glinted in his eyes. "You do have a way of speaking frankly. No, I don't run marathon races. I ski and I swim."

Of course. He'd been wearing a ski sweater the previous day, and there were ski slopes within a few hours' drive of Laguna Beach. Strange, she thought, that she should remember that particular detail, but it appeared the impersonal facts were the first to return. "Are you from around here?"

"No. From very far away." He eased her into a sitting position on the bed, then scooped up her legs and pulled back the covers so she could stretch out.

His grip was firm but gentle, every touch reverberating through Kim's senses. Even the air between them vibrated with subtle electricity, offering a promise of more intimacy to come.

She took a deep breath and tried to draw her thoughts back to the subject at hand. "You're from a foreign country?" she guessed. "Or when you said 'far away,' did you mean the East Coast?"

"You were right the first time." He busied himself tucking the covers around her. His fingers were strong and sure, lingering on her skin as if in a caress. "I'll explain in a minute."

"Jack." Kim cupped her hand over his, and felt a slight tremor run through him. "Please stop putting this off. Is it really so painful?"

He sat on the edge of the bed, his gaze troubled. "I'm afraid I may have landed you in a situation... No, never mind that. It's not as if I had a choice."

With a sinking sensation, Kim realized she had been hoping against hope that her husband would declare his love. But obviously he didn't feel any. In addition, his aura of watchfulness hinted at danger. Did the threat come from some outside source or from him?

Surely there was still time to annul the marriage. Kim's amnesia could be grounds for declaring the union void, since she was no longer quite the same person who'd walked down the aisle. But the whole situation seemed so bizarre, she couldn't help hoping for a reassuringly prosaic explanation.

"Why did you marry me?" She leaned against the pillows. "I need to know. Please don't try to coddle me."

Jack's eyes searched hers, and then he shrugged. "All right. I married you because I need an heir."

It was the last answer she'd expected. Wealth, beauty, even an alliance between two powerful families might make some sense, but an heir? "You wanted a baby machine?" she asked in disbelief. "You can hire women for that. They're called surrogates."

"But they wouldn't have your genes," he said.

Kim stared at him blankly, her mind racing. Genes? What could there possibly be about her heredity that would cause this man to travel from another country to marry her? "I'm not pregnant now, am I?"

Dark lashes shaded his green eyes. "Unfortunately, no."

Those eyes were so much like her own. And her mother's, as well. Kim could think of only one likely reason. "Are we related?"

"Third cousins," he said gravely.

"But why..." Kim stopped, feeling a wave of dizziness—or maybe it was disorientation. "People don't marry just to have babies, and they certainly don't marry their cousins."

"I assure you, we're far enough removed that there's no danger of inbreeding." Jack's fingers drummed the edge of the bed. "Your great-grandmother was the sister of my great-grandfather."

As he spoke, something came back to Kim. It surprised her that she should recover a memory so distant, but perhaps it was a good sign.

She visualized an old man with green eyes, and knew he was her grandfather. They were riding a Ferris wheel at a beachside Fun Zone, long ago, in sepia sunlight. He was speaking about a country called Lindelor, a tiny paradise in the Alps between Switzerland and Austria.

"I always thought I would go back." The longing in those long-ago words stirred a yearning inside Kim for a place she had never seen. "But I don't suppose I ever will."

His voice had had an accent like Jack's. Apparently this was more than a coincidence.

"You're from Lindelor," she told her husband. "Like my grandfather."

His head came up sharply. "Your memory's returning?"

"A little."

"Yes," he said. "I'm from Lindelor. As a matter of fact, I'm the prince."

The prince? Kim's mouth dropped open, but quickly she snapped it shut. The man must be pulling her leg.

"Does that make me a princess?" she joked. "Do I get a carriage? How about a fairy godmother?"

Amusement curved the corners of his mouth. "I'm afraid you'll have to make do with a car. And Hans Frick is the closest thing we've got to a fairy godmother. He's my foreign minister, and he's the one who found you in the first place."

That hawklike man in the doorway hadn't been a pastor but a government official. And the valet must be a real valet, not the car-parking type.

With a jolt, Kim realized what this meant. Jack was serious. She had met the foreign minister and his valet, so maybe he really was who he said he was.

Now that she thought about it, she did recall that Lindelor, like Monaco, retained a royal house. That meant it had a prince.

Prince Jack. Or using the name on the marriage license, Prince Jacques.

"I don't get it," she said. "If you needed an heir, I'm sure you could have had your pick of ladies, not just the granddaughter of an emigré. And why on earth would *I* have married *you?*"

She didn't accept the obvious explanation, that this was the best-looking man a woman was ever likely to come across, that he had the broad-shouldered build of an Olympian and that every time his eyes searched hers, she felt as if he were touching the most intimate parts of her body. In this day and place, that might be enough reason to have an affair, but not to get married.

As he weighed his answer, white teeth pressed against his lower lip. Bars of sunlight played across the sculpted power of his jawline and over his muscular chest.

She wondered if he knew how devastatingly attractive he was, then realized that of course he did. But he didn't seem to be stuck on himself.

"Do you want the real answer?" asked Prince Jacques. "Or something romantic?"

"I'm not a romantic type of person." Even in a mental void, Kim knew that to be true. "Just give it to me straight, Buster."

He laughed. "All right, Princess Kimberly. And I'm well aware that you're not romantic. You didn't marry me for my title or my irresistible charm, either. You did it for a million dollars."

"Excuse me?"

"I offered you a million dollars," he said. "And for that amount, you agreed to marry me, have my baby and then send us both back to Lindelor while you get a divorce."

Chapter Two

Kim's sense of unreality deepened. Wildly, she considered summoning a nurse or demanding to see a lawyer. The man was obviously some sort of trickster.

But he'd been here the night before with her family. Or at least, she had believed those people were her family.

"That's not possible," she said. "I wouldn't have sold myself for a million dollars. In fact, this whole business is ridiculous. I'm going to call the nurse and ask *her* if I'm the princess of Lindelor."

"She'll think you're crazy," Jack advised. "As far as the public knows, I'm in Los Angeles on routine business. We've kept the marriage as quiet as possible. Do you want the press dogging every step you take?"

What he said made sense, but it could have been subterfuge, too. "I wouldn't have married you," Kim said. "I would never wed a stranger and I would never agree to give up my child."

"Not even to save your country?" Jack slanted a mocking smile at her. It was the kind of smile that made her want to kiss him and slap him at the same time.

"Save my country?"

"From an evil villain, no less."

"Oh, please!" Kim threw her hands in the air. "It sounds like one of those loony adventures Donald Duck and his nephews are always getting involved with in 'Ducktales.'"

"You watch cartoons?" asked the man with the aristocratic cheekbones and the unnerving green eyes.

"I suppose I must. But that's beside the point." Kim refused to get sidetracked. "And what do you mean, save my country? America is my country, and it doesn't need me to save it. It's got the Marines."

"You must watch a lot of cartoons, if you remember Donald Duck when you still can't recognize your own parents," murmured Jack. He bent toward her, his expression half mocking and half tender. His tantalizing scent drifted to her nostrils, hinting of rumpled sheets and cast-aside clothing.

If she spent much time with this man, she would either end up throwing pillows at him or pulling him into bed beside her, right here in the hospital. "I don't *know* whether I watch a lot of cartoons and I don't care. Now quit changing the subject!"

He grinned, obviously enjoying her annoyance. "All right, I'll explain about our country."

"*Your* country," she insisted.

His expression sobered. "All right, my country. If the royal family of Lindelor fails to produce an heir, the country will come under the jurisdiction of Zakovia, our neighbor. A country whose ruler leaves much to be desired, I might add."

"So?" said Kim. "Produce an heir with somebody else."

"The Treaty of 1815 is quite explicit." He rubbed

his thumb along her cheekbone. The contact felt surprisingly intimate, Kim discovered as she caught her breath. "The prince—or princess—must marry someone of royal blood to produce a qualified heir."

"No ordinary babies need apply?" Kim challenged. "Come on, Jack, if this is really necessary, why don't you pick some third cousin who lives in Lindelor and dislikes the Zakarians or Zookersnookers or whatever they are as much as you do?"

"We've had this conversation before, you know," he said. "Before you agreed to the marriage. We discussed it at length."

His low tone gave her a chill. Kim pulled the covers tighter around herself and tried not to think about how much warmer it would be if he slipped in beside her. "And—and what was your answer?"

"There are no other unmarried females of royal blood in their prime childbearing years," Jack said, lightly tracing her nose with the tip of one finger. "I'm sorry to say it so bluntly, but it's true."

"That seems so unlikely. I mean, that there isn't *anyone* else."

Jack drew his hand away from her face, as if only now realizing that he'd been stroking her. Appearing troubled, he paced to the window. "I had always expected to marry my cousin Angela. She's ten years younger, so I had to wait until she grew up. Last year, we were on the point of announcing our engagement when she ran her motorcycle into a tree."

Kim's hand flew to her mouth. "Oh, the poor thing. Was she killed?"

"Happily, no." Jack turned to face her. "But she suffered serious pelvic injuries."

Kim glared at him. "And she can't produce your

precious heir, so you abandoned her virtually at the altar? Don't you have any feelings?''

Surprise flickered across his face. ''It wasn't like that. We were to have a marriage of convenience.''

''On your part, maybe!'' Kim's heart went out to Angela. She could imagine a young girl, awed and eagerly anticipating her marriage to this gorgeous prince, suddenly losing the man of her dreams as well as her ability to have children. ''First this innocent girl falls victim to some horrible accident...''

''Not entirely innocent, at least not when it comes to responsibility for the accident,'' said Jack. ''She was doing wheelies.''

''What?''

''On her motorcycle,'' he said. ''That was after she went off a ramp and jumped over three parked cars, two bicycles and a baby carriage. There was no one in the baby carriage, of course.''

''You're putting me on.''

''She shouldn't have added the wheelies afterward, because she had too much momentum. She was trying to set a new Lindelorian record and she succeeded. I think that compensated for the pelvic injuries, and losing me as well.'' He shot Kim a mischievous look. ''If you doubt me, come back to Lindelor and I'll introduce you.''

She might like to visit the land of her forebears someday, but not right now and certainly not as its princess. Kim wasn't sure what sort of life she normally led, but she knew instinctively that she lived it on her own terms.

''Look, I'm sorry I agreed to this crazy idea,'' she told Jack. ''It must have made sense to me at the time, but I could never deliberately have a baby with the intention of giving it away."

"It's a bit late to back out now." From his pocket, he drew a folded sheet of paper and handed it over.

It was a photocopy of a contract. Scanning it, she confirmed the terms he had explained: that she would marry him, have a baby and give it up in return for one million dollars.

The exchange of money was to remain confidential, she noted. Apparently she hadn't wanted her family to learn of it. She wondered if she'd told them about the temporary nature of the marriage, either.

The signature on the bottom was hers—or so it would appear. "Do you have a pen and paper?"

"Will this do?" Jack retrieved a pencil and pad from the bedside table.

Taking the items, she wrote out the name Kim Norris, then compared the signatures. They were identical.

Obviously, she had signed this document and accepted the sum of one million dollars. But why had she needed it?

In any event, she couldn't possibly fulfill the terms now. Whatever mind-set had persuaded Kim that she could hire herself out as a surrogate, it had vanished along with her memory.

She doubted the contract would hold up in a court of law. A woman couldn't sign away her rights to her own body, or at least she didn't think so. Still, it would be unethical to cheat the man.

"I'll give back your million dollars," she said. "You'll have to find some other way to produce an heir."

Jack pressed his lips together grimly as he regarded

her. Long moments passed, and Kim thought she perceived a gradual dimming of the sunlight.

"Well," he said at last, "I hope at least you'll allow me to try to change your mind."

"How would you do that?" As soon as she asked the question, she realized the man had an entire portfolio of techniques at his command. She only hoped he didn't realize the effect his touch had produced on her senses.

"To start out, by telling you more about Lindelor's history." His gaze swept her, as if he wanted to say more but then thought better of it. "Not right now, but as you heal. You might even discover a certain sense of patriotism."

She shook her head. "It would be one thing if I became pregnant by accident and gave it up because I couldn't take care of it, but to have it deliberately…"

"There's no reason you couldn't visit the baby," Jack pointed out. "Even share custody. I'm not requiring that you cut off all contact. Give me a chance, Kim. I deserve more than a summary dismissal."

The playful amusement of a few minutes earlier had vanished. Before her stood a man arguing for the future of his country.

In those shadowed eyes and the tight set of his jaw, Kim saw centuries of Lindelorian history merging into a single person. She could picture Jack as a swordsman in colorful garb or an archer targeting an approaching army from behind a screen of trees.

He had been born a prince, carrying royal tradition in every cell of his being. He would fight for his heritage with all the cunning and courage he possessed. But this was one battle he couldn't win.

"You can tell me as much as you like about Lindelor," she murmured. "In fact, I'd enjoy hearing about it. But as soon as I get out of here, I'm going to pay back the money and get an annulment."

From where he stood by the window, Jack watched her thoughtfully. He seemed to be debating something, and then at last he nodded as if reaching a decision.

"All right," he said. "But I insist on behaving as your husband and taking care of you until the money is returned."

Behaving as your husband. If only that were possible, just for the space of a fantasy and without any repercussions.

Kim wondered what part her attraction to Jack had played in her agreeing to a temporary liaison. She believed—or thought she believed—in true love and lifelong fidelity and two parents raising children together. But it was as if Jack truly came from another world, a land of green forests and youthful dreams, where stolen moments of happiness were worth a lifetime of regret.

She was going to have to keep her imagination in check, Kim reflected with a sigh. Especially since this man might be living with her until she remembered where she'd put the money.

It would be more sensible to stay with her parents while recuperating, but Jack clearly wouldn't accept being thrust out of her life. Anyway, she didn't suppose it would take long to withdraw the money from the bank or wherever she'd stashed it. Then she'd be free of him, if not of her fantasies.

"All right," she said. "You can behave as my husband in every way but one."

JACK ENTERED THE HOTEL suite quietly. He preferred to attract as little notice as possible when he moved about. A man never knew what he might overhear or who he might have a chance to observe.

The expansive living room had been transformed into an office, with most of the couches replaced by desks. The place bristled with computers, fax machines, a color copier and a bank of telephones that did everything but call him up in the morning and whisper sweet nothings in his ear.

Hans Frick, the foreign minister, was seated at one of the desks with his back to the door, talking on the phone over a headset. Nearby, Pierre Zerbe, Jack's private secretary, was tapping information into a computer.

On the one remaining sofa, Ladislaw Munchen lay reading a copy of the *Wall Street Journal.* Jack supposed that, as Hans's aide, Ladislaw generally performed his duties well, but he wished the man would soften his perpetually sullen expression.

From the kitchen came a tuneless hum and the slightly scorched smell of Siegfried Merkle's iron. Even in this land where polo shirts and safari shorts were considered the height of fashion, the valet insisted on pressing Jack's wardrobe to perfection.

Although Lindelor maintained a trade mission in Los Angeles, an hour's drive away, Jack had set up this temporary office close to Kim's home. He'd transformed dozens of hotel rooms just this way over the years, and now, inside the climate-controlled space, he could hardly recall whether he was in Singapore, Cairo or California.

As prince, one of Jack's primary duties was to enhance his country's trading position and promote its best-known products: pharmaceuticals and medical devices.

Even though their goal in coming here had been to secure a royal wife, Jack and Hans were making the most of this opportunity to broaden business contacts. This very morning, before going to visit Kim, Jack had attended a breakfast meeting with a major hospital corporation and put in an appearance at a medical convention.

Now, Pierre Zerbe spotted him and hit the save button on his computer. The private secretary, who had a sunny disposition to go with his blond hair and blue eyes, tugged at his carefully knotted tie and flicked a bit of lint off his tailored jacket. "How goes it? Has she agreed to carry on with the marriage?"

"No—she's determined to have it annulled." Jack paced across the carpet. "Don't worry. I'll win her over."

"How do you expect to accomplish that? With your legendary continental charm?" teased his secretary. "These American women have minds of their own."

"You mean, unlike Angela?" Jack chuckled. "Believe me, I know plenty about independent women. But Kim hasn't found the money yet. My first step, seeing as I'm her husband, will be to move in with her."

"In that, er, smallish unit of hers?" queried Pierre with a lift of the eyebrow.

Jack shrugged. "A man has to be prepared to sacrifice for his country. Besides, I doubt we'll be there long. I intend to take her back to Lindelor as soon as possible."

"You're very confident," said the blond man. "I hope for our country's sake that you're right."

Hans finished his phone call and regarded them both through narrowed eyes. Thin and silvery, with an aquiline nose and a guarded manner, he had a taste for subtlety and a talent for making advantageous business deals. Jack relied on him implicitly.

"The real problem is not Miss Norris—excuse me, the princess—nor the size of her apartment," the foreign minister reminded them both. "It is not even the matter of her consent, since she gave it once and may well be persuaded to give it again."

The problem, as they'd discussed several times since the wedding, was whether what had happened in front of the hotel had really been an accident or whether someone had deliberately chased Kim in front of a car.

If so, there could be little question who it was: agents of Zakovia. According to the Treaty of 1815, the clause regarding a takeover would be nullified if Zakovians were in any way linked to the death of the ruler of Lindelor or his heir. But the treaty said nothing of the ruler's wife. Until Kim produced a child and secured the succession, her life was at risk.

This office and its busy fax machines were a testament to why Zakovia coveted its neighbor. Thanks to the discovery in 1830 of medicinal hot springs with seemingly miraculous powers, a lucrative business in pharmaceuticals had sprung up in Lindelor.

While the mountainous Zakovia focused on agriculture and later heavy industry, Lindelor had invested in clinics and research. During World War II, as Zakovian youths fought on the side of the Axis powers, neutral Lindelor welcomed an influx of highly educated refugees, many of them doctors and scientists.

The result was that today the Zakovians suffered from a shrinking economy, with little to offer besides a modest ski resort, a handful of farms and underfunded plans for a casino.

Lindelor, on the other hand, sported a wealth of light industry and clinics in its tiny but productive eighteen square miles. Its per capita income was among the highest in the world.

"What have you found out?" Jack asked. On the couch, Ladislaw lowered his newspaper to listen.

"As you know, this whole business with the wedding was supposed to be a secret." Hans grimaced. "It was not. My sources in Zakovia aren't well enough placed to have learned any details, but apparently the government was well aware of who, when, where and why."

"The question now," said Jack grimly, "is how."

"A spy?" Pierre asked.

Hans shrugged. "As you know, in a country as small as ours, it's difficult to keep a secret. But the arrangements with the hotel were made at the last minute. You'll recall we took advantage of a cancellation, and only intimate members of the bride's family were notified."

"Seems to me almost any good hacker could have found out," grumbled Ladislaw, creasing his newspaper with irritable strokes. "Pierre charged the blasted thing on a credit card."

"I wasn't thinking," the secretary admitted. "It never occurred to me—but of course, we won't know what really happened until the princess recovers her memory."

"That should happen soon enough." Jack thought of the bits and pieces already returning to Kim, from her grandfather's origins to that nonsense about cartoons.

"In the meantime," Hans said, "I believe we should post security around the princess's apartment. An armed guard must accompany her everywhere."

"Absolutely not." If there was one thing Jack trusted, it was his intuition. Always keenly attuned to body language and vocal inflections, it had gone into overdrive where Kim was concerned. "That's guaranteed to make her get an annulment as soon as possible."

"You haven't told her yet that she's in danger?" asked Pierre.

"I advised hospital security," Hans said. "They've got a guard patrolling her floor."

"To answer Pierre's question, no. I decided it would only worry her needlessly." Jack didn't like deceiving Kim. Something about her openness elicited a similar impulse in him, but a lifetime of playing politics had stood him in good stead.

Winning her had been a difficult and uncertain matter. He'd sensed from the beginning that the slightest complication might tip the odds in the other direction. But withholding the truth made his responsibility to protect her all the greater.

"I'll be with her as much as possible," he said. "When I'm not, I'll arrange for someone else to be there—Pierre or you, Hans. And of course Siegfried will be staying with us. I doubt the Zakovians would try anything flagrant. Murdering a Lindelorian princess on American soil would create a diplomatic mess. The United States doesn't look kindly on terrorists."

"You think they would try to stage an accident." Hans nodded. "Which is why I'm so uneasy about what happened at the hotel."

"Perhaps we could rent a nearby apartment," suggested Ladislaw. "That way Pierre and I could keep an eye on things."

"Oh, that won't make her suspicious at all," scoffed the blond secretary. "The first time she sees us, she'll figure the whole thing out."

"He's right," Hans said. "We're going to have to play this low-key."

Jack suppressed a shudder. Kim's tiny, cluttered apartment was located down a narrow side street half a block from the beach. The area teemed with tourists and surfers. Danger could hide in plain sight.

He wished he hadn't had to involve her in this business of producing an heir, although it would have been a shame if they'd never met. There was something fresh and vital about Kim that had attracted him at once, perhaps by its contrast to his own guarded, circumspect life.

The attraction was entirely unexpected. In his thirty-four years, Jack had escorted beautiful women throughout Europe, but mostly he was known for his business acumen and diplomatic finesse.

This twenty-eight-year-old gamine with reddish blond hair seemed, by contrast, almost provincial. Southern California born and bred, she occasionally attended the theater and visited art museums, but mostly she enjoyed such unsophisticated activities as swimming at the beach, taking walks and reading popular novels.

Still, whether it was the unique experience of staring into green eyes as fathomless as his own or because of her innate honesty, Jack had felt connected with Kim from the moment they'd met.

Hell, he felt a lot more than that. Just the sight of her bright face and self-assured stance, hands on hips and head cocked at him skeptically, raised an instantaneous and unmistakable male response.

He'd made a point of keeping his distance, knowing his courtship depended on maintaining the pact that they would be intimate only as much as was needed to produce a baby. Even then, he was prepared to go along with artificial insemination if she insisted.

But every time he touched her, Jack felt a keen awareness jolt through him. He'd done his best to disguise his feelings and he didn't think Kim had noticed. Still, he'd been hoping they could conclude their business as swiftly as possible, before she realized she had a husband who wanted very much to engage her in the *real* sport of kings.

Yet he couldn't allow himself to court her in the truest sense. Delightful as a union might be in the short run, it would eventually prove a disaster. In every aspect of their upbringing and personalities, they were opposites.

The responsibilities of a princess would preclude Kim's continuing her career, which she loved. Her cherished independence and spontaneity would have to yield to tradition and duty. Sooner or later she would rebel, with consequent embarrassment to the entire country of Lindelor.

Jack preferred to do his duty as quickly as possible, before any unsuitable feelings had a chance to grow between them. And before his hunger for her overwhelmed his good judgment.

Two phones rang at once. As Hans grabbed one and Pierre the other, Jack decided it was time to make his getaway. Kim was being released from the hospital tomorrow morning, and he wanted to inspect the area around her apartment.

As he turned to leave, Ladislaw uncoiled from the couch and strolled toward a computer. For an instant, their eyes met and then Ladislaw's gaze flicked away.

The contact had been cool and unreadable. The aide was one man on whom Jack's intuition had never worked.

Possessing an inscrutable demeanor was an asset to a trade mission, not a liability, the prince reminded himself and headed for the door.

THAT EVENING, when Kim told her mother and aunt Valerie that the prince would be moving into her apartment, they both regarded her dubiously.

"Of course, he *is* your husband," her mother said. "But I don't suppose he has much experience as a nurse."

"Or with living in small apartments," Valerie declared.

"It might be best if you stayed with us," said her mother. "At least until you're back to normal."

"But that's the point." Kim was beginning to feel comfortable with these people, although she still wasn't sure she remembered them from before the accident. "I want to be in my own home. It seems like the quickest way to restore my memory."

Most important, she thought, it might help her to remember where she'd put the million dollars. Until she found the money, she was honor bound to tolerate Jack's presence.

Valerie and her mother conceded the point, despite a few grumbles, on condition that they be allowed frequent visits. "I'll be happy to cook if you need me," said her mother. "I'm not sure what they eat in Lindelor these days, but the traditional delicacies were deers' tongues and chocolate-covered grasshoppers."

"Ick," said Kim. "Maybe I'll just send out for pizza."

Valerie smiled as she and Kim's mother prepared to leave. "I don't think they really eat that stuff anymore."

The next morning, Jack provided a dove-gray skirt and jacket and a cowl-collared blouse for Kim to change into. It was probably one of her best business suits, not the sort of thing she would have chosen to wear home from the hospital. She supposed that people in Lindelor were accustomed to a more formal manner of dressing.

Then, when Jack escorted her downstairs, she found his valet seated in the back seat of an elegant European sedan.

"I'm a perfectly competent chauffeur," said Siegfried Merkle as Jack handed her into the front. "But the prince used to race and he insists on doing the honors himself."

The man had twinkling eyes and a cheerful, self-possessed air. Under other circumstances, Kim might have enjoyed his company, but what on earth was he doing here?

"You're just going to unpack his clothes, right?"

she hazarded. "I mean, you weren't planning on staying with us, were you?"

His eyebrows formed twin arches. "Why, yes. The prince couldn't function without me. Don't worry. I'll sleep on the couch, and you'll hardly notice I'm there."

"If you're sleeping on the couch, then where is he going to—" Kim stopped. Jack *was* her husband, but she hadn't counted on sharing a bed.

She forced herself to keep silent. Even as a temporary princess, she sensed that certain arguments should be private. Besides, she wanted to focus on their surroundings, in the hope of restoring her memory.

Anyway, maybe her apartment had two bedrooms. She couldn't recall.

Jack gunned the motor and they shot out of the hospital parking lot and down a long driveway. The car vroomed onto Pacific Coast Highway, with only a tiny slowing in recognition of the red light.

"That's illegal!" she said. "You could get a ticket!"

Jack favored her with a cocky grin. "I have diplomatic immunity."

"How rotten!"

"I try not to take undue advantage." He shot around a panel truck.

"Did anyone ever tell you you're reckless?"

"It runs in the family," he said, and flashed through a yellow light the instant before it changed. "There, that wasn't illegal."

Siegfried leaned forward from the back seat. "Pardon me, princess, but everyone drives this way in Europe."

"Even little old ladies?" Kim asked.

"Especially little old ladies."

She tried to distract herself by studying the coastline to her left—what she could see of it between the buildings. Dotted with tiny sailboats, the Pacific Ocean sparkled in the sunlight. Near the horizon, Kim thought she detected an island.

Santa Catalina.

It was coming back! Excitedly, she gripped the armrest and scanned the town they were rapidly approaching. Low, cottagelike shops sported handlettered signs and shingled roofs. The terrain itself was hilly, offering intriguing vistas as the land sloped toward the beach.

Glancing inland to where the ground rose steeply, she noticed that some of the hills bore blackened patches, partly hidden by overgrowth. There must have been a fire here, but not too recently, she thought.

She remembered nothing of it. And she didn't recognize the art galleries lining the road or the restaurants or clothing shops.

I don't even know what I do for a living, Kim thought in dismay. *Do I have a job? Is there a boss I should be calling?*

The car slowed. Shifting her attention to Jack, she saw him watching intently as a couple of children roller-skated down a sidewalk toward the highway. He hit the brakes a moment before they shot into a crosswalk against the light.

Kim's heart pounded. If not for his caution, he would have smashed into those children.

Jack reached over and touched her hand reassuringly. "I'm only reckless with my own safety." He waited until the children were clear of the road before starting up.

The brief contact made Kim's breath come faster— or maybe it was just a reaction to the near tragedy. But there was a masculine confidence about Jack that made her feel both protected and uneasy at the same time.

She wished they had met under other circumstances. Maybe they would have enjoyed each other's company, at least for a brief flirtation. But given their differences, it seemed unlikely that it would have lasted.

Jack eased forward a few more blocks, then turned left onto a narrow street leading toward the ocean. Kim felt her muscles tighten in anticipation as she read the name of the street.

It didn't sound familiar. Scarcely a block long, it ended at the beach, but halfway down Jack turned the car into an alley.

He stopped behind a panel truck. The car blocked a garage door bearing the sign We Shoot Illegal Parkers, So Move It!

"The natives sound hostile," said Siegfried.

"That garage is half Kim's," Jack explained. "Besides, I'll move the car in a few minutes."

"I hope Pierre has unloaded the truck," said the valet. "He may not have your cavalier attitude about getting shot."

"That's *your* truck?" Kim asked in dismay. "What on earth is in it?"

"Just a few necessities," said Siegfried.

Jack came around and helped her out of the car. Rising stiffly, Kim swayed against him and felt a tickle of electricity run up her hip where it brushed his muscular thigh.

What on earth was wrong with her? And how did the man manage to radiate so much heat in the cool, breezy air?

"Let's get you inside," he said. "You'll be safer there."

She wondered at the urgency in his voice. There was nothing dangerous about a little salt air. The doctor this morning had advised against exercising for a few days, but he hadn't said anything about having to stay indoors.

Still, she did want to see her apartment. It was the first step toward normalcy.

The prince escorted her up an outside staircase to the second floor and opened the door. Kim caught the frame to steady herself as she took a shaky step inside.

Sunlight poured through sliding-glass doors on the far side of the living room, where a balcony gave a partial view of the ocean. The room itself seemed dim by comparison to the bright daylight, even when Jack switched on a lamp.

Slowly Kim's gaze traveled from the worn shaggy carpet to the frayed couch, past an overstuffed and lopsided bookcase to a framed poster advertising *The Phantom of the Opera*.

This, apparently, was home. But as far as she could tell, she might as well never have been here before.

Chapter Three

"Your Highness?" A blond young man with an easy smile stepped out of the kitchen. "Welcome home."

"This is Pierre." Jack helped Kim to the couch. "My private secretary."

"He—he isn't going to stay here too, is he?" She knew she must sound rude, but she couldn't imagine where all these people would fit. It was obvious at a glance that this apartment hadn't a square foot to spare.

"Have no fear," said Pierre. "I'm just moving in Siegfried's cooking gear, his ironing equipment and so forth." He gestured toward a rack of men's clothing crammed against one wall. "And a small selection of Prince Jack's raiment."

The valet followed them inside and exchanged greetings with the secretary. "Everything appears to be in order."

"We didn't need to have extra phone lines put in, as it turns out," Pierre told Jack. "The princess already has a fax in her bedroom."

"I do?"

"Yes, and your answering machine is full of messages." Pierre gave her a small bow. "I could transcribe them, if you wish."

Kim shook her head. "I'd better listen to them. They might jog my memory."

"Mostly, you need to rest." Jack escorted her through the living room, skirting a collection of suitcases, and into the bedroom.

One bedroom, Kim noted. And one double bed. Well, maybe the luxury-loving Prince Jack would change his mind at bedtime and move to a hotel. It was a dim hope, but she clung to it.

In the bedroom, a second rack of men's clothing was jammed to one side. Next to the bed, a small table held an answering machine and a small fax copier. On the floor sat a briefcase the size of a laptop computer.

If all this stuff is mine, I must need it for my work, Kim reflected. *I wonder what I do.*

She wished her brain wasn't so arbitrary, recalling general facts but refusing to summon up personal ones. "I just need to listen to—"

Jack scooped her up, and before she could summon a protest, he laid her on the bed. "You've had enough exertion for one day, my dear bride. Time to rest."

He held her a moment longer than necessary, his arms making intimate contact with her body. When he released her, the feel of him lingered on her back and legs.

"There's so much to do." Kim tried to sit up, but her muscles defied her. She *was* still weak, even though it annoyed her to acknowledge it.

Her husband sat beside her, one hand stroking the hair back from her bruised forehead. A faint throbbing, which had troubled her all morning, eased beneath his touch. "The important thing is for you to recover your strength."

"So I can act as a baby machine?" She realized how churlish that sounded. "I'm sorry. I didn't mean it that way."

His eyes, so disturbingly like her own, rested on her face thoughtfully. "It must be hard for someone who wasn't born into this position to understand. Kim, I haven't merely placed duty above my own wishes. The truth is that I've never even considered what my wishes are. It would be a useless exercise."

"But once you have an heir, you'll be able to relax a bit, won't you?" she mused. "Then, what would you do with yourself?"

He gave her a startled look. "I've never thought that far ahead. Keep promoting my country's trade interests and spend a lot of time with my child, I suppose."

"But wouldn't you want to find someone to love?" Kim's eyelids were drooping, but she wasn't ready to end this conversation yet.

She didn't know what she expected him to say, certainly not that he felt the same crazy attraction that was flaming through her nervous system. Besides, a wild physical response wasn't exactly the same as love.

His mouth twisted ruefully. "I may be a prince, but I don't believe in fairy tales. My primary responsibility will always be the security and well-being of my country."

"But it sounds as if your problems will be over once you have a child."

Jack shrugged. "One hopes so. Still, Prince Igor of Zakovia is a hard, ambitious man."

"Does *he* have an heir?"

"Yes, and a rather nice young fellow he is, too," Jack said. "But Igor is only in his fifties. It will be a very long time before Grand Duke Kristoffer ascends the throne."

"These countries seem so far away," Kim admitted. "I can't really absorb the fact that I matter to them."

"You matter very much indeed." Jack regarded her intently. "You agreed to make this noble sacrifice to save fifty thousand good people from a dark future. They will be forever in your debt."

Kim suppressed a twinge of guilt. It wasn't her fault the nobility of Lindelor had failed to produce enough daughters. "The only debt I'm interested in is the million dollars I owe you."

"Just get some sleep. We nearly lost you once, and I don't want that to happen again." Jack bent over her, his lips tracing her forehead. It was odd how his kiss soothed and stimulated her at the same time.

Just before she dozed off, it occurred to Kim that if she ever did yield and keep her original bargain, giving up the prince might turn out to be as great a sacrifice as giving up the baby.

THE PHONE WOKE HER. Someone had turned off the ringer but forgotten to lower the volume on the answering machine.

"Kim?" came a man's voice. "It's Hank Richley. I was sorry to hear about your accident, but the office said you're home now. Give me a call about my listing on 1201 Pinecrest, would you?"

While she was debating whether to pick up the phone, the caller clicked off.

Apparently she had clients who called her at home, Kim reflected. But what kind of business was she in?

The most important thing she needed to know was where she'd put Jack's money. With luck, it would turn up right under her nose.

Tentatively, as if she were going through a stranger's room, Kim examined the nightstand and the bureau. She found her checkbook and savings book almost at once, tucked into a corner of the top dresser drawer.

There was a little over $500 in her checkbook, and no record of any large sum being deposited and then disbursed, either. The savings account boasted $3,257.18.

She was only a little over $996,000 shy of a million, she thought.

A tap at the door was followed by Siegfried Merkle's kindly face poking in. "I thought I heard a noise. You're awake, eh? How about some soup?"

With a shudder, Kim recalled her mother's comment about deers' tongues. "What kind of soup?"

"I've made fresh chicken noodle," said the little man. "I double as a cook while traveling, as you can see. But if you prefer, I could open a can of split pea or some clam chowder."

"Chicken noodle would be fine."

Half an hour later, Kim had eaten and dragged herself through a shower. It felt wonderful to blow-dry her hair and watch it spring to life. And the bruises on her face had faded to the point where they could be hidden with makeup.

Pulling on a sweatshirt and jeans, she went in search of Jack. He didn't appear to be in the apartment, and Siegfried was humming loudly as he ironed in the kitchen. So loudly that he didn't hear when Kim slipped on thong sandals, opened the door and stepped outside.

A calendar in the bedroom had indicated this was March. Although the breeze felt cool, the sunlight fell warmly about her shoulders.

Below in the alley, two girls in shorts and shrink tops whizzed by on in-line skates. Kim wondered if she knew either of them, but neither acknowledged her.

Kim frowned, and immediately felt a faint throb of headache. She considered going back inside for some pain medication, but the risk of getting waylaid by the valet was too great. She wanted to walk around unaccompanied, listening to her inner voice and making her own observations.

It was hard to believe, standing here in this unremarkable setting, that she was a princess. If she'd worn a crown or had a knot of photographers accosting her it might have seemed more credible. In fact, Kim realized, she didn't have a clue what behavior was expected of her.

But then, she reminded herself as she walked slowly down the steps, she wasn't going to be a princess for long.

At ground level she hesitated, wondering where Jack had gone. He appeared to have a lot of business to conduct on behalf of his country.

What a strange, complex man he was. Kim suspected she must be accustomed to a different sort of fellow, easygoing and taking life as it came.

Moving cautiously, she proceeded toward the beach. Several people jogged past, paying her no attention.

The air was tangy with salt and—surprisingly— vanilla. Sniffing, Kim spotted a small bakery up by the highway. Sometime she would have to go in and see if she recognized anyone.

Today, though, she felt a strong urge to view the ocean. Resuming her snaillike trek, pausing for breath every few minutes, she covered the remaining yards to the beach.

As soon as she cleared the buildings the Pacific Ocean spread before her, calm despite a few wind-whipped waves. A half-dozen children were building a sand castle off to her left, while a man walked his leashed collie along the waterline.

What a peaceful scene, she thought. No wonder she could tolerate such a tiny apartment, when it gave her proximity to the ocean.

The light glaring off the sand forced her to blink several times before she grasped that she wasn't imagining the dark dots against the water a hundred or so feet out. From their sleek, arching movements, she concluded that they must be sea lions.

To her right, taking advantage of a slight swell, half a dozen surfers rode the waves. In their wetsuits, they gleamed the same shade of black as the sea lions.

But there was something else moving through the surf, a man's figure cutting through the low waves with smooth, powerful strokes. A casual swimmer herself, Kim recognized the speed and grace of an athlete.

The man was still way out in the water, heading toward shore. Kim wondered how far he had swum before turning around. From the masterful way he handled himself, he might have gone a considerable distance.

As the man drew nearer, she made out tightly muscled shoulders and a head of brown hair. There was something fierce, almost feral about the way he thrust through the waves. He put her in mind of a wolf, plunging across arctic waters in pursuit of its prey.

Come to think of it, the waters must be darn near arctic today. Kim didn't see any other swimmers.

The man reached the shallows and stood, shaking water from himself with swift, impatient motions. His nearly naked body was a classical display of perfect proportions.

Then his head came up and his gaze fixed on Kim. The expression on his face shifted from watchfulness to alarm. She glanced around, half expecting to find a dune buggy bearing down on her, but all she saw were children playing and people sunbathing.

Stalking forward, Jack cleared the water and reached her at a lope. "Who let you out?"

"You mean, off my leash?" Kim tried to ignore the overwhelming immediacy of the man, his bare chest and slim hips looming toward her. Only a wisp of a swimsuit prevented a full assessment of the crown jewels.

He took a deep breath as if willing himself to calm down. "You might get dizzy. You're still recuperating, you know."

He had a point, but Kim hated to yield. "The apartment felt stuffy. It's crowded with all those clothes and things." Not wanting to sound pettish, she added, "But Siegfried was very kind. He makes good chicken soup."

"He should have come with you."

"I didn't tell him I was leaving," Kim said. "It didn't seem like a big deal. I've only gone a block."

Jack reached out to catch her elbow. "You might have collapsed."

"Somebody would have called the paramedics." Kim deliberately spoke with more confidence than she felt. She refused to allow herself to be smothered.

A tiny inner voice whispered that it might be fun to let this man pamper her. What would be wrong with door-to-door chauffeuring, a protector always at her side, a private chef, a castle in the mountains, satin sheets...

The thought of a bed, and specifically the much-too-cozy one in her apartment, brought Kim crashing back to reality. Jack only wanted her until she produced an heir. Allowing herself to become dependent on him would be setting herself up for a fall.

She pulled her elbow from his grasp and saw him flinch at the implied rejection. To smooth it over, Kim ran her palm across his droplet-covered biceps. "Aren't you freezing? Where's your towel?"

Immediately, she realized her mistake. The man wasn't cold; he radiated heat like a blast furnace. And touching the corded bulge of his upper arm had a disturbing effect on her nervous system, on the order of plugging herself directly into an electrical outlet.

How on earth was she going to survive a night in bed with him?

"I didn't bring a towel." Jack stood motionless beneath her touch. "I'm used to the cold. Lindelor is in the mountains."

"How do you people get warm?" she murmured. "Lots of blazing fires?"

"And hot springs." The man's breath came quickly, belying his calm demeanor. "Other than that, I expect we keep warm the same way you do."

The electrical impulses inside Kim began emitting sparks all the way down to her ankles. Tiny bursts of heat made her nipples tighten, and she was grateful for the sheltering folds of the sweatshirt.

She was letting her physical reaction carry her away, Kim told herself, closing her eyes to regain her bearings. What Jack wanted to remove were her genes, not her jeans. If she valued her future peace of mind, she would never forget that.

Strong arms encircled her. "Are you all right?"

Taking a deep breath, Kim opened her eyes. She found his face only inches away, his mouth hovering near hers and the hard planes of his face blocking the horizon. "I was just thinking."

Soft breath teased across her cheek. "About heating systems?"

"The natural kind," she admitted.

His lips touched hers lightly, as if savoring the moment. The ache in Kim grew almost unbearable. With the tip of her tongue, she tantalized his mouth, urging him to plunge deeper.

His arms and body went rigid. With his half-naked body tight against hers, she could feel the instantaneous male arousal.

He stepped back abruptly, as if he'd been burned. "I suggest we get you home. You're still weak and confused."

Kim didn't feel confused, just frustrated, but there was no point in arguing. The man could be immovable as stone when his defenses sprang up. "All right, Your Highness. Let's go."

AS HE PULLED A T-SHIRT from his canvas bag and slipped it over the swimsuit, Jack kept a surreptitious watch on the beachgoers around them. He'd experienced a moment of panic on emerging from the water, to discover Kim alone and unguarded.

He should never have left the apartment without making certain someone was watching her. His mild-mannered valet had too many other duties to serve as a reliable watchdog.

Maybe Ladislaw's idea of renting a nearby unit wasn't so bad, after all. Jack supposed he should have given it more consideration, but he had an instinctive mistrust of any suggestions that came from the swarthy, closemouthed aide.

That didn't mean there was anything wrong with Ladislaw, who'd worked as Hans's assistant for the past three years. He simply had a dour presence and an abrupt manner that rubbed Jack the wrong way. As long as that didn't bother the foreign minister, the prince would not interfere.

As they made their way off the sand, Jack had to fight the impulse to slip his arm around Kim's waist. With her slim build and halo of reddish blond hair, she seemed so fragile that he wanted to physically take charge of her.

It wouldn't do, of course. She resented any attempt at protection. Besides, allowing himself to make physical contact was proving a test of Jack's self-control.

The moment he'd spotted her from the water, he'd become keenly aware of the desirable shape half-hidden beneath her loose clothing. Kim had a feminine way of moving and a sensuous self-awareness that aroused him more than any woman he'd ever known.

But it wasn't his intention to take advantage of her,

not beyond the requirements of duty. Once she resumed the agreement to have his baby, he would make love to her tenderly, but withhold any real passion that might mislead her into believing she meant more to him than she did.

They were approaching the alley, with Kim breathing hard from the uphill climb. After making a quick survey of the street for any threat, Jack suggested they pause to rest.

Kim sucked in the air, ducking her head in embarrassment at her weakness. "You know, I don't think I can make it up those stairs right now. And no, I won't let you carry me. Let's stop at the bakery."

She indicated a coffee shop a few doors farther, at the corner of the highway. Battling an instinct to lock her away, Jack gave a nod of assent.

I mustn't make her feel like a prisoner.

To tell the truth about her danger would mean to reveal that Jack had always known Prince Igor might act against her. The discovery that he had deliberately withheld this information might ruin his chances of winning her back.

"It smells terrific," he said as he escorted her across the street. "Do you eat here often?"

"I don't know," she admitted. "But it seems like a good idea to find out. Aren't odors supposed to be a powerful stimulant to memory?"

"Then by all means, let's indulge." Jack shouldered open the door amid the jangle of bells.

Except for a dining area to their right, the store was cluttered with merchandise: packets of potpourri, hand-carved wind chimes, bags of fat-free cookies, books on vegetarian cuisine. Directly ahead, doughnuts, muffins and cookies filled a glass counter.

"Yo, Kim!" said the long-haired fellow behind the counter. "Long time no see."

She regarded the man doubtfully. "I, uh, was in an accident. I'm afraid I've temporarily lost my memory."

"No kidding?" The young man cocked his head curiously. "You mean, like, you don't know who I am?"

Kim shook her head.

"What a trip! I'm Choco," he said. "I've been working here for two years."

"Choco?" Jack wondered if it would be impolite to ask the derivation of such a strange nickname.

"It's really Charles," the clerk volunteered. "But when I was a kid, I put chocolate on everything I ate. Say, are you her brother? You've sure got the same eyes!"

"Cousins," Jack said. "Tell me, what does the lady usually eat?"

"A maple doughnut with chocolate sprinkles and vanilla-flavored coffee," said Choco.

"Sounds good," said Kim.

"I'll have the same."

To their right stood half a dozen small tables, all empty at this hour. Escorting her to a seat and stowing his bag beneath the table, Jack returned for the food. He was pleased when Choco disappeared into the kitchen immediately afterward.

Business was apparently scarce at this time of the afternoon, and Jack hoped it stayed that way. Setting the food down, he slid into a chair and watched Kim expectantly.

"What?" she asked, stirring cream and sugar into her coffee.

"You mentioned the potency of smells."

A maddening grin quirked across her countenance. "You're certainly in a hurry for me to recover and get on with this business. Anxious to return to your ski slopes? Or—let me guess—some special lady?"

Although he maintained an air of informality with his staff and his subjects, Jack was accustomed to a certain subtle acknowledgment of his position. Being teased about girlfriends, even by his wife, bordered on cheekiness.

He had to remind himself that cheekiness was an American trait. Even after spending a year at a New York university, and visiting the country numerous times on trade missions, Jack could never get used to the national insistence on equality in all things.

Still, he had no desire to chastise Kim. "I've dated many women, but there's no one in particular."

She nibbled at her doughnut. "Why not?"

Jack had never given it much thought. "I suppose because I always assumed that I would marry Angela, when she was old enough."

"Did *she* assume it?"

"Well, of course." Actually, Jack's relationship with his young cousin was more like that of brother and sister. He had supposed they would simply accommodate the requirements of marriage as Lindelorian royalty had done for generations, without any silly insistence on personal fulfillment. "She knew from childhood that she was destined to be my wife."

Kim rested her chin on the palm of her hand. Her eyes took on a dreamy quality that made Jack want to run his finger along her cheekbone. "I can't imagine living like that. I was brought up to follow my heart."

"And yet, at the age of twenty-eight, you assured me your heart was unengaged," Jack pointed out. "Wouldn't you eventually have decided to settle down with some suitable man in order to have a family?"

Kim blinked. "You mean someone I didn't love? Of course not. As a matter of fact..." She stopped.

"Go on!"

"It seems to me I never gave much thought to having children. So when you suggested getting married just to produce an heir..." She stopped, frowning. "I was starting to remember, but it's fuzzy."

Jack decided to fill in the rest. "You said at the time that your maternal clock, whatever that is, hadn't started ticking and might never. You considered that perhaps you might spare yourself the misery by bearing me a child, and then you could go your merry way unencumbered."

"I said that?"

"Not in so many words," he admitted. "But you are rather wedded to your career."

"Which is what?"

"You're something called a title rep." Jack didn't want to discuss her job, since he was in no hurry for her to resume it, but he couldn't hold back everything. She would get the facts sooner or later. "I believe it involves real estate."

"Title rep." Kim let the words roll around in her mouth. "Rep must stand for representative." She recalled the message on her tape earlier. The caller must have been a real-estate agent, since he'd mentioned listing a property. "Oh! We insure the title to houses, offices, land, that sort of thing."

"The title?" Jack considered himself knowledgeable about business, but as far as he knew there was no need to take out insurance on a company name. Even in the highly regulated United States, one simply checked to be sure it wasn't already in use and then registered it.

Excitement brightened Kim's face. "It's coming back! 'Title' means the legal right to a piece of real estate! When people buy a house, for instance, they have to be sure the person selling it really owns it. And that it isn't tied up in a lawsuit or co-owned by someone who doesn't want to sell. That's what I do! I sell them title insurance and my company researches the ownership and issues the policy."

The doctor had been right; her memory was coming back. But would she recall everything, or would some matters remain blacked out? "Remember anything else?"

She bit her lip, her small-boned face solemn in concentration. "Some general stuff about real estate. And I can kind of picture my office. But not the people I work with. And nothing about my personal life. How frustrating!"

"Give it time," he said.

She made a face, then smiled at her own childishness. Filtered through hanging plants, the sunlight cast a warm glow over her luminous skin. At this moment, Jack didn't care whether she had amnesia. He only wanted to create new memories with her, lots of them.

But he must not let himself get distracted from his duty to Lindelor. Or from the need to protect Kim, either. "The most important thing you could recall would be what happened after the wedding. How you came to be injured."

Her reaction was instantaneous and unpremeditated. Her mouth clamped shut, her eyes narrowed and her shoulders hunched protectively. "No. No, I can't!"

Reaching across the table, Jack stroked her arm. "Relax, Kim. It was just a suggestion."

"I can't remember and I don't want to!" Her voice quivered.

The doctor had warned that traumatic events might be lost forever. Obviously, whatever had happened at the wedding reception had been very frightening for Kim, which intensified his suspicion that she'd been attacked.

It would be useless, maybe even harmful, to pressure her. "It's all right," he murmured, wishing he could pull her into his arms and kiss the fear from her face. "Really, Kim."

"Is it?" She stared at him pleadingly. "Jack, why am I so terrified? Look at me. I'm shaking."

He lifted her hand and kissed the palm. Her skin smelled lemony, with a hint of vanilla. Rebelliously, his body tightened at the scent and he was nearly overwhelmed by an impulse to trail kisses up her arm.

He must not think of his own desires but of his duty. Stiffening his back, Jack drew away. Kim regarded him with disappointment and a trace of hurt, quickly disguised by a stubborn lift of the chin.

"Now that I've remembered what kind of work I do, I should listen to my messages and visit the office," she said. "I work on commission, so I can't afford to take much time off."

"You're in no condition to go to work!" he blurted. "A few minutes ago, you could barely walk."

"That's because I've been spending too much time in bed." She had changed before his eyes from a hesitant girl to a hardheaded businesswoman. "I've got a lot of catch-up work to do. And I need to track down the money I owe you."

As he drained the last of his coffee, Jack forced himself not to argue. He needed to salvage what little he could from the conversation. "I have one request."

"Yes?" The single word bristled with suspicion.

"Indulge me by allowing someone to accompany you wherever you go." As her mouth opened to protest, Jack added, "There's still the possibility of a relapse. You could become lost and confused. Why take needless chances?"

The clamor of bells drew his attention sharply to the door. With relief, he saw that the new arrival was an elderly couple.

Reminding himself that, in any case, Prince Igor of Zakovia was unlikely to send Uzi-toting goons onto American soil, Jack returned his attention to his wife.

"All right." Her face scrunched in an endearing expression of reluctant compliance. "I guess I don't have to be Superwoman."

"Thank you. And I shall endeavor to avoid playing Superman." As he rose to escort her out, Jack told himself that he'd made a major error by behaving too much like an ardent suitor. When he'd acted protectively, it had mobilized all her defenses.

He would have a hard enough time breaching Kim's battlements as it was. He must remain in the role of cousin and friend, and keep their discussions focused on the impersonal fact that Lindelor needed an heir.

It could only hurt his cause if Kim ever came to suspect that Jack was beginning to want all the pleasure and intimacy that usually accompanied the creation of new life. He must never let her know that he ached to be her husband in every sense of the word, at least for the length of their contract.

Chapter Four

After listening to the messages on her answering machine and talking to her mother on the phone, Kim found herself wearier than she had expected. Although aside from her head injury she'd suffered only cuts and bruises, apparently her body still needed time to regain strength.

Collapsing on the sofa, she watched "Duck Tales" and a couple of other cartoons while Jack made phone calls. One good thing about having amnesia was that she couldn't remember the plots, since she was sure she must have seen most of these episodes before.

The cheerful valet fixed them a dinner of minted lamb, fresh asparagus and couscous. The ricelike dish of steamed cracked wheat was, according to Jack, all the rage in Lindelor.

As she ate, sitting in her tiny kitchen across from the prince, Kim experienced a jab of regret at the realization that she might never visit her family's ancestral homeland. It would be fun to see the plazas her grandfather had described, with their inlaid stones and flower-filled planters, and to meet her daredevil cousin Angela.

She really would like to help the country out of its

dilemma, since Jack seemed to dislike the Zakovian ruler so much. But whether the accident had flipped some internal switch or whether Kim was merely getting in touch with her own long-dormant feelings, something inside her had changed, which made the pact impossible to fulfill.

The Kim of the old days, it seemed, had taken little interest in motherhood. She had deceived herself into believing that, by giving birth to a child for Jack, she could short-circuit her biological clock and remain free-spirited and unencumbered.

With her memory stimulated by the phone messages, Kim recalled how much she had enjoyed her work. Driving around the county, chatting and lunching with real-estate professionals, had been fun and challenging.

It wasn't just a job. She enjoyed getting to know a variety of people and being part of their lives. Sometimes she was a shoulder to cry on, or a cheerleader for the downhearted or a buddy to share the good times.

She earned a respectable living, and enjoyed setting her own schedule and acting spontaneously on her wishes and whims. She'd envisioned herself reaching middle age happily unattached like Aunt Valerie, a never-married magazine editor who served as her role model.

Now that her mind was humming again, bits and pieces of the past kept popping into Kim's mind. But the odd part was that she took less interest in the details of her work than in the family scenes—especially those that involved children.

She pictured the Christmas after her brother's first son, Vance, was born, with everyone gathered around the tree taking turns cuddling the baby. Then there'd been the birthday party—was it for Tim's younger son, Jason, or his daughter, Michelle?—during which the children had sneaked outside with their dessert plates and virtually coated themselves in chocolate frosting.

Her biological alarm clock might not have gone off yet, Kim supposed, but it was edging close to wake-up time. She knew with absolute certainty that once she had Jack's baby, she could not give it up.

Peering across the table through a screen of eye-lashes, she noted the moody way in which Jack was finishing his meal. Although he ate with exquisite correctness, European-style with the fork in the left hand and the knife in the right, he gave the impression of shoveling down his food without tasting it.

The man was obviously annoyed. He must have expected Kim to acquiesce quickly, once her memory started to seep back. No doubt he was in a hurry to return to his normal routines and surroundings.

Surely there must be some other woman distantly related to him, someone Jack and his retainers hadn't discovered yet. Kim tried to picture another lady with bright green eyes, whose legs would brush Jack's beneath the table and whose hands would run up those muscular arms as her lips drew near to his....

Catching his gaze fixed on her, she wrenched her thoughts back to the present. "Want some ice cream? I've always got some in the freezer." That was one of the privileges of living alone; you never had to worry about someone else snarfing down the last of the ice cream.

"If you like." He didn't radiate pleasure at the

suggestion, but at least one could always count on a prince to be polite, she thought.

Kim opened the freezer compartment and stared inside, momentarily disoriented. The usual handful of frozen dinners had been obliterated by package after package labeled with the names of different seafoods, meats and even pastry doughs.

"Where's my ice cream?" she demanded, afraid to move the packages for fear she'd never get them all crammed in again. "Probably at the very back!"

Jack stretched lazily. "Check the refrigerator. Siggy wouldn't forget dessert."

Grumpy at having her space invaded, Kim opened the lower door. Displaying themselves on her wire shelves were three deep-dish pies, a torte-style cake and a plate of molded flan topped with caramel sauce.

"This is *better* than ice cream," she said in wonder.

"A small sample of Siggy's talents." Jack managed a smile at last.

After losing a mental battle regarding her waistline and cholesterol level, Kim chose the flan *and* the torte. "I wouldn't want either of them to feel neglected," she explained as she set them on the table.

Jack fetched a knife, spatula, plates and forks. The dishes were rimmed with gold leaf and bore a royal crest in the center. The gleaming silver utensils bore a miniature version of the same crest.

This was one change that Kim didn't mind. Wherever Siegfried had stashed her plastic plates, stainless flatware and discount-store glasses, she could happily live without them for the next few days.

And that's all it would take, the way her memory was returning, Kim felt sure. By then, she would return the million dollars and send Prince Jack and his cook extraordinaire back from whence they came.

They could leave the food behind, though, if they wished.

After dinner, Jack helped clear the table but insisted on leaving the dishes in the sink. "Siggy would be offended if we washed them."

Never having to wash a dish again might almost make it worthwhile to be a princess, Kim mused, then remembered that even if they had a child, the agreement on both sides had been for a temporary marriage.

Well, the agreement now was for no marriage at all, as far as she was concerned. If only Siegfried had gone out for the night, she could plant Prince Jack on the couch and get some rest.

That hope collapsed like a parachute as soon as she emerged from the kitchen. There atop her well-worn sofa, draped in a comforter her mother had crocheted from leftover yarn, the royal valet lay softly snoring.

"He certainly looks comfortable," murmured Jack, checking to make sure the front door was locked.

"How long has he been with you?"

"Eight years," he said. "Since my father died."

"He gets passed down like an antique clock?" she asked.

"The Merkles have served the LeGrand family since the fourteenth century." He spoke so matter-of-factly, it was hard to absorb that he was discussing a relationship that had endured for more than six centuries.

"Did your mother have ladies-in-waiting and that sort of thing?" Kim whispered as they tiptoed across the room, so as not to wake the sleeping servant.

"She died when I was young, but yes, she did," Jack conceded. "Frankly, I'd always hoped my father would remarry and produce more children. It would have taken a burden off me."

Kim wasn't sure whether to feel flattered or offended at the realization that she figured into this burden. "Is there any chance that Angela will recover her ability to—you know?"

Flicking on the light in the bedroom, Jack guided her inside and closed the door behind them. The space seemed to shrink to the size of a children's playhouse, leaving barely enough room to move without bumping into each other.

"She has recovered, more or less. But having children would be very dangerous for her. Risk taker she may be, but dying in childbirth isn't on my cousin's agenda."

If he was trying to intensify Kim's guilt, he'd done a good job of it. She hoped her refusal to cooperate wouldn't force Angela into a life-threatening choice.

Kim forgot her concerns as Jack shifted past her and approached the rack of clothing. With smooth, unselfconscious motions, he shrugged off his ski sweater and slacks.

All that remained was a black slash of fabric no larger than that scandalously tiny swimsuit he'd worn at the beach. He offered an unparalleled vista of broad shoulders, golden skin, slim hips and long, muscular legs.

"Well?" he said. "Aren't you going to change for bed?"

Embarrassed at having been caught staring, she fetched her brushed-cotton nightgown from the closet and slipped into the bathroom. It was a tiny place, but at least it offered privacy.

Although the apartment was beginning to seem familiar again, Kim couldn't help seeing it afresh. The minuscule dimensions, pervasive dampness and occasional encounters with sand underfoot didn't seem like charming reminders of her proximity to the beach. They struck her as remnants of an adolescent life-style that she should have long outgrown.

When she came out, she saw that Jack had gotten into bed, still apparently wearing nothing more than his underpants. Doing his best to brace himself on one side of the double bed, he looked anything but relaxed.

No wonder he'd worn such a grim expression at the dinner table. He must not have been looking forward to tonight any more than she was.

Kim's fists clenched in defiance. Well, no one was forcing him to stay! If he chose to make himself uncomfortable, he had no one to blame but himself.

She certainly didn't intend to surrender one square inch of her half of the bed. If he could be stubborn, so could she. A double bed *was* meant for two people, anyway, wasn't it?

The drawbacks became apparent the moment she clicked out the light and slid under the covers. Her bare leg made instant contact with his, sending ripples of warmth washing across her body.

Gloomily, she reflected that a double bed was intended for two *intimate* people. Certainly not for two strangers, who wanted as little intimacy as possible.

How on earth could they avoid touching? It wasn't possible. They would simply have to do their best to ignore each other.

"How do you say good-night in Lindelorian?" she asked.

"*Bonne nuit,*" said Jack. "Or *gute Nacht.* Or, more commonly, good night."

"English is one of the official languages?" She'd never realized that.

"In honor of Smitty Mitchell." When she didn't respond, he added into the darkness, "He's the English healer who discovered the medicinal qualities of our spa waters."

"I see." Kim waited in vain for any further explanation. Obviously, the prince was not in a talkative mood.

Despite her earlier weariness, she found herself lying stiffly awake, listening to the sound of Jack's breathing. A faint glow from a neighboring houselight shone through the curtains and the lullaby of the surf ebbed and flowed.

"There's really no point in your being here," she said into the stillness. "You could go back to your hotel and enjoy all the comforts of home."

"I'm your husband." Hoarseness edged his voice. "I belong with you. Of course, if you'd care to accompany me..."

"No," she said.

In the silence that followed, Kim had nothing to focus on except the tantalizing sensations surfing across her nerve endings. The man made an indentation in the bed that rolled her toward him, almost forcing her to touch him, and she had to keep propping herself up. Even so, his subtle scent taunted her, whispering of pinewoods and hidden glades.

This reaction was purely a matter of two healthy young people being thrown together, Kim reminded herself. Other than being of compatible ages, she and the prince had nothing in common except some distant ancestors.

Not that she was immune to the variations on the Cinderella story that set teenage hearts racing. *Pretty Woman. My Fair Lady. Pride and Prejudice.* But they were make-believe. They didn't involve real princes, political squabbles and signed contracts worth a million dollars.

A million dollars that she hadn't found yet. But she would.

Beside her, Jack rolled onto his stomach. The motion upset Kim's delicate balance, dropping her into a warm trough and bringing her hip into jarring contact with his.

Not just her hip, either. The motion had flipped her onto her side, so that her entire pelvic region was angled toward him. Meanwhile, Jack, with nowhere to retreat, swung toward her with the unfortunate effect that the minimally covered area between his hips made electric contact with her most intimate region.

Warmth flared into scorching heat. Kim knew she ought to pull back, but gravity and a primeval urgency overcame her resistance.

The prince reached down as if to move her away, but his hands got no farther than the soft curve of her hips. And there they lingered, holding her tightly to the fire while his head shifted toward hers across the pillows.

Kim waited like a royal deer transfixed by the sight of the prince's arched bow. She felt his hands stroke up her back, crumpling and lifting the nightgown in the process, and then his mouth came down on hers with a low groan.

Her lips met his, parting invitingly beneath his probing tongue. She gripped his shoulders, her body measuring the length and power of him, her breasts crushed against his chest.

It was a fiercely intimate embrace, with contact flaring along her inner core. Kim felt herself falling into him, melting and merging, her softness molding itself to his hard shape.

His mouth released hers, traveling along her jawline and down her throat. His arms scooped her so that her back arched, offering her body to him like a banquet.

Nuzzling the loose-fitting gown from her shoulders, his lips trailed along her breasts. With tiny, demanding licks, he tasted first one nipple and then the other until Kim could barely restrain the need raging through her.

This was happening too fast. There could be no denying their physical attraction, but what would be left once she surrendered?

Jack was no compliant lover who would indulge Kim's wishes and share in her activities. Once he took her, she would become merely another subject of the prince. Every instinct in her rebelled at the thought of being conquered and then, as per their agreement, discarded.

With a shudder of regret, she pulled away. Jack froze, his body still curving as if to dominate hers.

"I'm sorry," Kim rasped. "This isn't a good idea."

"Idea?" he repeated. "Do you realize what we were doing? We're husband and wife, Kim. And we both want this. You can't simply put me out like a stray cat."

"Are you claiming your marital rights?" she demanded. "We have laws against that in California!"

A disbelieving laugh choked from him. "Excuse me. I was under the impression that what happened was mutual."

"Well, sort of." Sitting up, Kim hugged her knees. "It wasn't my idea for us to share a bed. Then you rolled over and—well, it isn't a very large bed, as you can see. But that's no excuse for trying to seduce me into getting pregnant."

She knew the last accusation was partly unfair. At least it had the welcome effect of startling Jack into sitting up, too.

"You think I was trying to manipulate you for my own purposes?" He ran his hands through his thick brown hair. "That isn't my style, Kim."

"I—I didn't really think it was," she conceded. "Look, why don't you and the Snoring Gourmet go back to your hotel? I'm sorry for what I said, but I— I guess I'm still pretty vulnerable."

She didn't like making a claim of feminine weakness, but she *had* suffered a serious head injury. Surely that accounted for her momentary loss of judgment.

"No." He swung his legs over the side of the bed. "I'm not going to the hotel, but I will sleep on the floor."

"I'll bet you never slept on a floor in your life!"

"Did you?"

"In a sleeping bag, once," she said. "On a trip."

He regarded her through narrowed eyes. "The carpet will do fine. It doesn't have sand fleas, does it?"

Kim bristled. "Obviously not!"

"Obviously?" he challenged.

"Well—your ankles aren't red and itchy, are they?" she returned.

"If they were, I certainly wouldn't broadcast the fact." With princely dignity, he stared into the semi-darkness and then dropped from sight, presumably to lie beside the bed.

Kim could no longer deny the guilt nipping at her brain. "Don't you want some covers?"

"It's not cold."

"You're hardly wearing anything," she pointed out.

"Cold air is refreshing."

"I thought it wasn't cold."

"It's warm in certain areas and cool in others," he muttered. "Go to sleep, Princess. I'll have a cot brought in tomorrow."

"And put where?" she demanded.

"Just go to sleep."

With a sigh, Kim stretched. She could feel the dent where he'd lain, still warm from his presence. Her breasts and hips retained the imprint of his embrace. She didn't see how she would ever doze off.

JACK CURSED HIMSELF for a fool. He'd yielded to his impulses like a schoolboy, treating the princess like any ordinary woman. Even though she might consider herself one, he did not.

She was his wife. And much as he needed to produce an heir, there had been no need to pounce on her like a wild animal.

He didn't understand why he'd responded to her nearness so strongly. He was, after all, reasonably experienced with women, and at controlling his impulses.

This entire episode troubled him. He had agreed that the marriage would be one of convenience and would last only as long as necessary. Further, he knew from observation that he and Kim were not suited to each other. Their world views, their approach to duty, their life goals were entirely incompatible.

Some women could rise from a life of unrestricted freedom to accept the responsibilities and restraints of a royal household, like Princess Grace of Monaco. There were others, as the British royal family had discovered to its woe, who would never adapt. Anyone could see that Kim was one of these women.

The floor was hard and uncomfortable, the carpet scratchy and the air, as Jack's passion receded, unpleasantly chilled. The experience reminded him of his adolescence in a military school. It was exactly the sort of discipline he needed to restore his sense of propriety.

Tomorrow, he would resume a more dignified courtship. Although the increasingly rapid return of Kim's memory might pose a threat to his plans, it might also aid him. She was a difficult woman to assess, Jack admitted silently.

He must appeal to her independent spirit, not treat her like a playmate. Only in that way could her reservations be whittled away and replaced by the delicate accord that had led them to the altar in the first place.

The pressure of the floor against his traitorous midsection reminded Jack, for one unguarded moment, of how close he had come to possessing a most desirable treasure. His hands cupped, feeling again the smoothness of her hips, and his mouth shaped itself for an instant to the perky resistance of her nipples.

He forced his thoughts onto arctic ice floes and the far outposts of space. No warm, beguiling flesh, no dark lashes against a lightly tanned cheek, no reddish hair fanned across the pillow.

Into the cold reaches of the universe floated Prince Jack, wondering for one treasonable instant if his country was worth the sacrifice.

Chapter Five

Kim awoke to the sound of the shower running. She blinked against the dim light, gray with the kind of early morning beach fog that burns off before noon.

As a recollection of the previous night rushed back, she felt a rush of dismay at her own susceptibility. The man was gorgeous, granted, but that didn't mean she had to abandon her good sense.

Stretching, she arose, her feet feeling a trace of warmth on the carpet where the poor guy had slept. He must be stiff as a surfboard, she told herself with a glint of sympathy.

With any luck, Kim could spare him further nights of discomfort. She just needed to turn up that darn money.

Clearly, she must have financial documents beyond a checkbook and a savings passbook. Since her memory for impersonal facts seemed to be returning, she posed herself a question: where else would a businesswoman put her long-term savings?

The answer came at once: in a mutual fund.

Earlier, she'd spotted a file box on the floor of the closet. Kneeling, she flipped through it. There were tax records, product warranties, insurance policies—and a file for a mutual fund!

With growing excitement, she lifted it out. Sitting on the floor, she began reading the statements.

The latest one was dated a week earlier and showed a small dividend. No wonder it was small. She had only invested about five thousand dollars.

Grimly, she stuffed the paper back in the file and shoved it into her closet. Along with frustration, she felt a growing uneasiness. Why was it proving so difficult to find the money?

She calmed herself with the thought that sooner or later her memory would return. Feeling a bit better, she padded out to see what Siegfried was whipping up.

Belgian waffles were on the menu today, Kim discovered. She'd have to take a long jog to work them off...once the doctor allowed her to resume exercising.

"These look delicious," she told the rosy-cheeked valet as he poured her coffee.

"Thank you, Your Highness."

"Could you not call me that?" she said. "I don't feel like a highness."

"I do understand about Americans and their sense of equality," the fellow beamed. "Would Mrs. LeGrand suit you better?"

"Just Kim," she said.

"Would you like me to rewash and iron your wardrobe today, Princess Kim?" he asked.

"My wardrobe?" Aside from a few business suits in dry-cleaner bags, most of what she possessed appeared to be jeans and T-shirts. "No, thank you."

"Then I'll vacuum and dust," he said. "I meant to do it when we arrived, but there wasn't time."

"That would be fine." Kim had to admit, the place could use a cleaning.

"I might touch up a few things, as well," the valet murmured, more to himself than to her, as he topped her waffle with strawberries and whipped cream. "Now that your memory is coming back, it's no longer necessary to keep everything exactly the same, is it?"

"Not exactly," she agreed cautiously. "But—"

Her objections died in her throat as Jack entered, his hair still damp from the shower. He wore a maroon velvet robe tied loosely at the waist, baring a good portion of his chest.

His face had a tight quality, as if from too little sleep or too much frustration or both. Why did he have to look so devastatingly handsome, even as his abrupt movements and terse comments to Siegfried advertised his grumpy mood?

They couldn't go on this way. She must locate the money and pay him off, today if possible. Then she could get back her privacy and he could return to the luxury to which he was accustomed.

Allowing a bite of waffle, fruit and whipped cream to melt in her mouth, Kim considered how best to proceed.

She had already decided that she needed to drop by her office this morning to do some catching up. With her amnesia disappearing like morning fog, she could even vaguely recall how to get there.

Then, since it was Saturday, her aunt might be home. Valerie had been her maid of honor. Kim assumed that if anyone knew why she had wanted the money and where she'd put it, her aunt would.

Across the table, Jack was reading a copy of the *New York Times*. Siegfried must have collected it early this morning from one of Laguna's newsstands.

"I have to run some errands today," Kim said. "There's no need for you to come." To forestall objections, she added, "I've got a phone in my car, so if I run into problems I can call for help."

The paper rattled as her husband lowered it. "You're hardly well enough to drive."

"People in Southern California are born with a steering wheel in their hands. I could do it with my eyes shut."

"Bravado aside, it takes tiptop reflexes to drive safely, *especially* in Southern California. I'll drive you myself."

His stern tone brooked no argument, but Kim was determined to give him one anyway. "You're not a prince around here. And I'm no longer an invalid. I'll be fine."

"Drive if you wish, but I'll ride with you." He returned his attention to the front page, indicating the issue was settled. Kim opened her mouth to argue and then thought better of it. Knowing Jack, if she refused he would simply follow her in his car, and what was the point of that?

Setting a jar of preserves on the table, Siegfried regarded his sovereign thoughtfully. "Your Highness, I've ironed your dark gray suit, but if you prefer the uniform..."

Jack snapped the paper down onto the table. "Siggy, I hardly think I'll need—" He paused. "Oh, that's right. I'd forgotten I'm touring a rehabilitation hospital this afternoon.''

Kim felt a wave of relief mixed with disappointment, which she quickly quashed.

''I would suggest the uniform,'' murmured the valet. ''It makes a good impression on the patients.''

''There, you see?'' Kim couldn't resist hammering home her point. ''You're otherwise occupied.''

''Not this morning,'' said Jack. ''And I'll arrange for someone else to accompany you this afternoon.''

''Absolutely not!''

He regarded her with barely restrained exasperation. ''May I remind you that the doctor has not yet approved your driving? And you're still taking pain medication. Suppose you were stopped by a member of the constabulary?''

That was a point Kim hadn't considered. The previous night before bed, bothered by residual pain from her injuries, she'd taken a prescription pill that contained codeine. If any of the narcotic remained in her system and she happened to be pulled over, she would be treated the same as a drunken driver.

''Oh, all right, someone can drive me,'' she grumbled. ''But only for today.''

''I'm glad you know when to accept help,'' Jack said evenly.

Kim suspected that if the tables were turned and he was ill, the prince would be the world's most unwilling patient. But she gritted her teeth and kept quiet.

After breakfast she phoned Valerie, who explained that she had a hair appointment in the morning but wanted to invite Kim and Jack for a late lunch.

''Jack has a commitment, but I'll be there with whoever's baby-sitting me,'' Kim said. ''Thanks,

Valerie. I've got some important questions to ask you."

"By all means," said her aunt. "I'm delighted that you're feeling well enough to get about."

Then, with Jack at the wheel and her briefcase tucked into the back, Kim set off for her office in nearby Mission Viejo.

The title company was located in a discreetly landscaped shopping center, the tile-roofed Spanish-style buildings nearly hidden by a screen of trees. Although it was Saturday, she found the front door open and several people at work.

As heads turned and smiles broke out, Kim wondered what she'd told these people about her marriage. She wished there weren't still nagging details that refused to come clear. It made her wonder what other secrets were lurking in the back of her brain like time bombs.

With a blink to clear away a slight sense of dizziness, she recognized her boss, Alan Morales. He gave her a hug, then pumped Jack's hand. "The newlyweds return! You know, Kim, you swore you weren't taking a honeymoon, but we all figured you'd change your mind. At least we were prepared for your absence, but I'm sorry you didn't get to enjoy it more."

"Thanks," she said. "But I need to keep my work up-to-date."

He waved away her concerns. "Your regular clients are very loyal. We're crediting you with their commissions."

"She hasn't received doctor's approval to go back to work." Jack studied the office with professional detachment, taking in the up-to-date computer and communications equipment. "I'd prefer she rested a while longer."

"I couldn't agree more." Alan stepped aside as several other workers came to extend their congratulations and express concern for Kim's condition. "Besides, she's got a husband now, and I'm sure you're perfectly capable of supporting her until she's better. By the way, what is it that you do, Mr. LeGrand?"

Kim swallowed hard. Obviously, she hadn't told these people about Jack's being a prince.

"I'm in the export business," he said without missing a beat.

"Agricultural products? Technology?" Alan probed.

"Medical equipment and pharmaceuticals."

"Great line to be in!" Her boss returned his attention to Kim, and they began reviewing the details of her pending deals.

THE PRINCESS'S MEMORY was returning a little too quickly for Jack's taste. Watching her with her employer, he could see there were gaps in her grasp of details, but often she supplied facts as if plucking them from midair.

He supposed that sooner or later she was going to recall the details of her accident. If she figured out that she'd been attacked—assuming that she had been, of course—she'd be furious at having been kept in the dark about the danger. Who could blame her?

But at this point, leveling with her would be a risky course. Realizing that the threat would continue through her pregnancy could only reinforce Kim's resolve to end this alliance before it passed the point of no return.

As long as she didn't find the money, however, Jack suspected that her integrity would prevent her from annulling the marriage. It might not force her into his bed, but the previous night had indicated that sooner or later she was likely to succumb.

He frowned at the thought. The accusation that he had set out to seduce her had stung. Never would he wish to impregnate a woman against her will, even if she did yield to him in a moment of weakness.

If only they could spend more time alone together, without her worrying about business and family and friends. He felt sure she would agree to have the baby, just as she had before.

On the other hand, he still wasn't sure what she needed the million dollars for. He doubted that she wanted it for herself. Listening to Kim talk with her boss, he could tell the woman was highly competent in business and well able to provide for her own future; nor did she seem the type who coveted yachts and Rolls-Royces.

"Listen," Alan said as the two of them finished. "I've got a great idea. The snow level's down to six thousand feet in the mountains. I'd be happy to lend you my cabin up at Big Bear. Why don't the two of you get in some skiing? You've been threatening to try it, Kim. Between my wife and my grown kids and me, we have plenty of equipment. And you deserve a real honeymoon."

Mountains. A cabin. Skiing. Jack hadn't realized there was anything so appropriate nearby. "How long does it take to get there?"

"Two hours," Alan said.

"We can't." Kim shook her head firmly. "I've got a doctor's appointment Monday. And until he gives me permission, I'm not supposed to exercise."

"I hadn't thought of that." Alan looked crestfallen.

"Perhaps a bit later in the week," Jack suggested.

The manager brightened. "Sure! I'll write down the directions and give you my spare key."

"No!" Kim touched the man's arm lightly. "Really. I doubt we'll have time."

She was planning to get rid of him quickly, Jack could see. It seemed the best tactic to yield, at least for the time being. "I bow to my wife's judgment. Thanks very much for the offer, though."

He and Kim walked into the sunshine together. She wore a smile of relief, although whether it came from resolving her business concerns or from avoiding a trip to the mountains with him, Jack couldn't be sure.

He wished he could cancel his tour of the rehab center, but he understood some of the patients were of Lindelorian descent and eagerly anticipating the visit. And clearly Kim was anxious to see her aunt and unwilling to postpone the meeting.

Jack had wrestled all morning with the problem of who should accompany her. Not that he suspected anyone on his staff of disloyalty, but he wasn't sure any of them could restrain Kim if she took it into her head to do something foolish.

Besides, whatever threat might lurk, it was likely to appear in disguise. Her guard needed to be watchful, discreet and if necessary ruthless.

The only one he trusted completely was Hans. And while the foreign minister had planned to go to the rehab center with the prince, he would of course consent to escort the princess instead.

"So," Kim said as she rode home, "what did you think? I suppose my office looks small, compared to what you're used to."

"It's very up-to-date," Jack pointed out. "With modern technology, you don't need a huge office and a lot of equipment anymore."

"Diplomatically put," she said. "Jack—would you please slow down?"

"Must I?" He was finding the going rather tedious. The streets and stoplights were so well-engineered that driving required little of his race-driver acuity. Now he hit the gas and darted around a slow-moving truck.

"That wasn't necessary." Kim pointed to a freeway ramp a short distance ahead. "We're going to turn off the street, anyway."

"But it was fun." Jack grinned at her. "If you like stodgy driving, you'll be happy this afternoon."

"Is Siegfried really that bad?" she asked.

"Not Siegfried. Hans."

"Hans?" She studied him in dismay as the sports car whipped along the ramp. "The foreign minister of Lindelor is going to play chauffeur? Honestly, Jack! What are you thinking? It's a waste of the man's time."

"Oh, he'll enjoy the change of pace." He only hoped the afternoon *would* prove a waste of Hans's time.

JACK HADN'T BEEN kidding. Hans was the pokiest driver Kim had ever ridden with. The thin, hawkish fellow piloted the sedan along the four-lane highway as if afraid the wind would dent the bumpers if he went over 30 mph.

It wasn't more than a few miles from Laguna Beach to Valerie's house in Newport Beach, but at this pace they might not arrive until dinnertime, she grumbled silently.

Kim told herself she ought to be relieved that at least Jack was wending his way separately to the rehab center. Every hint of his scent and accidental brush of his body reminded her achingly of the night before.

She supposed she shouldn't have been so hasty in turning down Alan's offer of his cabin, if the doctor gave permission. For years, Kim had been promising herself to learn to ski. And her strength was flooding back.

But the very thought of finding herself alone with Jack in an isolated setting sent quivers of apprehension down her spine. They might not have to share a bed, but the night-and-day intimacy could prove her undoing. The previous night she had seen how weak her willpower was.

Kim's thoughts returned abruptly to the road as they passed the turnoff to Newport Center. From the drive on their right, a speeding car ran the light and shot straight toward them. Kim caught a glimpse of a blond woman at the wheel, her eyes hidden behind sunglasses.

At the same time, she realized, a heavy truck was coming abreast of them on the left, about to block their escape. Hans needed to change lanes and stomp on the gas, but his reactions were too slow. For a heart-stopping moment, he seemed unable to respond at all.

"Floor it!" Kim shouted.

At the last possible moment, the speeding car to

their right swerved off the road, narrowly avoiding a collision as it tore along the shoulder and screeched to a stop. From nowhere, a police car had materialized behind it.

To their left, the truck roared past. It hadn't slowed at all, as if unaware of the crisis.

Hans let out a long breath. "I don't know where he came from." Kim wasn't sure whether he was referring to the speeder, the truck or the policeman who had so providentially appeared.

"If the cop hadn't showed up, I think that idiot would have hit us." She uncurled her hands, which had formed such tight fists that the nails left indentations in her palms. "What a maniac. She must be drunk."

Hans was still breathing hard as they stopped at a light. "I'm afraid I'm not used to California drivers."

"The drivers here are among the most courteous in the world!" Kim flared. "We have to be, or we'd have permanent gridlock. Do you want me to drive the rest of the way?"

The foreign minister's lips pressed together in determination. "Thank you, Your Highness, but no. I've never failed in my duty."

They turned off Coast Highway a short time later, wending their way onto the Balboa Peninsula and then over a bridge to Lido Isle. On both sides, sailboats filled Newport Harbor and bobbed at their moorings. Large homes with glass walls lined the harbor on both sides.

"I must say, this is an attractive area," observed the foreign minister. "I thought your aunt was a magazine editor. They must be better paid here than in Europe."

"She owns three trade magazines," Kim explained, pleased that the detail had popped into her mind. Almost everything was becoming clear—except what she most needed to know. "But she couldn't afford one of these homes by herself. She co-owns it with a married couple—teachers—who spend their vacations traveling and a family from Argentina who come here in the summer, when it's winter at home."

"An interesting arrangement," sniffed the minister.

It might seem a bit unorthodox, Kim reflected, but house sharing wasn't uncommon in the beach area, where real-estate and rental prices were staggering. She supposed a great many things about her world seemed odd to the Lindelorians, just as their country would to her.

But then, she wasn't likely ever to visit it except on a guided tour. The thought gave her stomach a twist. How would it feel to stand in a group of tourists, staring at the palace and knowing that Jack lived there with some other woman? And that he had become forever a stranger?

Disliking this turn of mind, Kim directed Hans along the streets named for Mediterranean cities. A few blocks later, they arrived at Valerie's house.

Two stories high, it was set back only a few feet from the street and took up nearly an entire lot. Houses pressed cheek-to-jowl, their Italian designs giving the feel of a Riviera community. Or so Kim imagined.

Hans surveyed the street before exiting the car. He frowned at Kim, who had already emerged from the passenger side unaided.

"The princess should at least allow me to hand her

from the car," he observed. "It is protocol, although it may seem old-fashioned to an American."

With the sea breeze tickling her nose and the sound of gulls overhead, Kim felt her heart expanding after the past week's confinement. She even felt generous enough to wish the rigid foreign minister could relax a bit.

"Mr. Frick," she said, deciding that the use of first names might be presumptuous, "as I'm sure you know, I have no intention of continuing as princess. But I respect the fact that you're only doing your job."

"I am doing more than my job." Hans pushed the buzzer on the gate that separated Valerie's property from the street. "I'm doing my sacred duty. And I do hope, Your Highness, that you will reconsider your decision to abandon your ancestral homeland."

"But do you hope this because you're concerned for my niece's welfare or because you are heedless of it?" The no-nonsense female voice came from inside the gate, where Valerie had materialized. Tall and much more regal in bearing than Kim could ever hope to be, her aunt swung open the gate and smiled at them both.

"How nice to see you again, Miss Norris."

"Valerie!" Kim ran into her aunt's arms. The unfamiliarity from the hospital had vanished. This was her father's sister, the woman she'd turned to with her adolescent problems when even her parents hadn't been able to understand.

Walking through the yard arm in arm, Kim could recall the excitement she'd felt as a young girl visiting her aunt. Here she had met magazine writers, politicians, artists, models and businesspeople. It was

Val's serene and uncomplicated enjoyment of the single life that had convinced Kim that she, too, should never tie herself down by marrying.

The past was rushing back, she realized. Soon, she hoped, the remaining blank spaces would vanish.

Hans strode past them to hold the front door. He made a courtly half bow, his eyes lingering for a moment on Valerie's face.

Well, well, Kim thought. *He likes her. But then, who wouldn't?*

Inside, they bypassed the formal living and dining rooms for a glassed-in terrace, where a table had been set for lunch. Valerie's longtime housekeeper appeared, bearing a tray of tea sandwiches and cut vegetables and a pitcher of iced tea.

Valerie plied Kim with questions about how she felt and kept her and Hans amused with stories of the antics of various musicians at a recent benefit concert the magazine had sponsored for a shelter for the homeless. Only when they had finished the sandwiches and were nibbling at cheesecake did she bring up the subject of Prince Jack.

"Has he accepted your change of heart?" Valerie asked.

Kim had told her family before she left the hospital that she had reconsidered her marriage. But she still wasn't clear exactly how much her aunt knew. "Could we talk privately?"

The foreign minister regarded them disapprovingly. "Your Highness, I have explicit directions not to leave you unattended."

"But she would be with me." Valerie fixed him with a steady gaze. "Are you afraid she'll seize the chance to run out the door, Mr. Frick? Is my niece being held captive?"

"Not at all." He drew himself up. "However, the prince considers her to be in a confused state as a result of her accident. She may not be thinking clearly."

"Or do you mean she may not be thinking the way you want her to think?" Valerie inquired.

"We believe the princess should not be subject to, shall we say, unpredictable influences until she has quite recovered herself."

"Unpredictable influences?" Valerie gave a dry chuckle. "My niece has been confiding in me since she was a young girl. I hardly consider myself a loose cannon, Mr. Frick."

He brushed a crumb from his trim mustache. "Miss Norris, as a spinster I hardly think you are in a position to advise the princess about her marriage."

For a moment, Valerie simply stared at him. Then she burst into peals of laughter. "A spinster? Do you picture me as some sort of Victorian recluse? I know quite enough to advise my niece about men! As a matter of fact, I've lived with several of them. Honestly, Mr. Foreign Minister, you seem to be the one who's behind the times! You and your wife must move in very restricted circles."

"I've been divorced for many years," he said coldly. "And I see nothing amusing about my having presumed that you possess certain traditional virtues, Miss Norris, even if you do not seem to value them."

"Virtues?" she responded, her face alight with amusement. "Oh, I assure you, I've never been noted for my virtues!"

Hans's face flamed. "I'll wait in the other room, then." With a stiff bow, he retreated.

Valerie's eyes met Kim's, and they fought to stifle their laughter. Finally Kim laid her face on her arms and shook for a few minutes.

Gradually her composure returned, hastened by the realization that she had urgent business to conclude. "Valerie, how much do you know about my marriage?"

Her aunt's expression sobered. "You told your parents and me that you were marrying Jack out of concern for your homeland. Something about him needing an heir. It didn't hurt, I presume, that he's incredibly good-looking."

"Did you know—" Kim bit her lip, then forced herself to proceed. "Did you know that we had agreed that after I had a child, we would divorce?"

Her aunt drew a deep breath. "You admitted that to me right before the wedding. You were having second thoughts."

"Did I tell you he was paying me a million dollars?" Kim held her breath.

Valerie twisted her napkin in her lap. "You mentioned a large sum, but not how large. Kim! I can't believe you would be tempted by that."

"Neither can I," she admitted miserably. "Oh, Valerie, I don't want to continue this charade, but I have to pay him back. I haven't got a clue where I put the money. I was hoping you'd know."

Through vents in the glass enclosure, a breeze carried the heady scent of roses to them. A few houses away, Kim could hear children shouting gleefully as they played. They were such ordinary aromas and sounds, part of the world to which she was increasingly anxious to return.

"I have no idea," Valerie said. "You never told me."

Chapter Six

"But you must have some idea!" Kim hugged herself against the light breeze. "Where did I usually put my money?"

Her aunt began absentmindedly stacking the dirty dishes. "The same sorts of places I put mine, except that you don't own any real estate yet. Some in the bank, some in mutual funds. Surely you have the papers at your apartment."

"I looked." Kim felt frustration returning. "So far, no luck. Valerie, why would I have needed that much money badly enough to marry Jack for it?"

The housekeeper appeared in the doorway, and Valerie didn't answer until the woman had departed with the dishes. Then she said, "I'm sure you knew, as we all did, that your father's business has suffered some serious reversals."

Kim searched her memory. "He—he develops computer software and games for CD-ROM, doesn't he? But that's all I remember."

Her aunt tucked a wisp of hair into her French twist. "A few years ago, your father decided to branch into hardware as well. He bought the patent to a new gaming device that attaches to computers and gives virtual-reality effects. But there was a lawsuit over the rights, and by the time that was settled he lacked the capital to go into production. Now he's facing bankruptcy unless he finds an investor.''

"Maybe I gave the money to him!" That would explain a lot. Kim could well imagine she might have married Jack under those circumstances. It must have made sense to her, until the accident changed her perspective about giving up the baby.

"He wouldn't have accepted money from you," Valerie corrected. "I suppose you might have had some idea of investing through a third party, so he wouldn't know where the money came from. Since you bought your mutual funds through my financial adviser, you might have gone to him. I'll get you his phone number."

As her aunt hurried off, Kim tried to quiet her uneasiness. If she'd invested the money with her father, she couldn't exactly yank it back.

Still, once she knew where it was, she could make some intelligent decision about how to proceed. Perhaps she could transfer ownership of the investment to Jack. He would eventually recover his money and even make a profit when her father's business turned around.

Valerie returned a moment later with the adviser's business card. Hans followed her into the room.

"The princess appears tired," he said. "His Highness insisted I bring her home in time for a nap. I believe you have a dinner engagement."

Kim groaned inwardly. She didn't want to sleep; she wanted to call the adviser. But he wasn't likely to be in his office on a weekend, anyway.

"Very well. We're having dinner at my folks'

house tonight and I don't want them to see me looking haggard.'' She stood and hugged her aunt. ''Thanks, Valerie. Thanks—a million.''

When Valerie extended her hand to Hans, he lifted it to his lips and kissed it, with deliberate slowness. The tall woman gave a start at the unexpected caress.

''I can't tell you what a pleasure this has been,'' said the foreign minister.

Valerie wore a bemused expression. ''I hope we haven't been rude, exiling you from our conversation.''

''Perhaps you would atone by accompanying me to dinner tonight,'' said the foreign minister, to Kim's astonishment.

''I'd be delighted,'' said her aunt. ''Kim, do close your mouth. At forty-five, I'm not turning in my dancing shoes yet.''

''I didn't mean—I just—'' Kim smiled. ''Have a good time.''

EVERYTHING HE HAD FEARED was coming true.

Standing on the balcony of Kim's apartment, Jack stared through a scattering of palm trees toward the beach. Hans's account of the near collision on Coast Highway sounded like anything but an accident.

The other vehicles had probably been fortified to protect the drivers. Kim would almost certainly have been injured and possibly killed if that policeman hadn't shown up and pulled over the onrushing car.

Jack needed to take her away from here, but she wouldn't go willingly. To complicate matters he'd received an invitation for them both to a ball tomorrow, sponsored by the Zakovian tourist office in Los Angeles.

Zakovia didn't maintain a formal West Coast consulate, so its tourist office filled that function. The ball was being held in honor of Prince Igor himself, who was in town to speak at a foreign-affairs council round table on the New Europe.

Jack ground his teeth, oblivious to the cheerful late-afternoon shouts drifting toward him from a beach volleyball game. He wouldn't put it past that old goat to try to kill Kim, although not at his own ball. Still, Jack loathed the thought of letting her anywhere near his country's nemesis.

Now in his late fifties, Igor had left his heart in the era of absolute monarchy. Exercising near total control over his tiny country, he lavished its modest income on his own pleasures rather than investing in the economy and coveted the much greater wealth of his neighbor.

If Kim died—or rejected Jack utterly and permanently—Lindelor would still remain independent until Jack's death. But as its heir apparent, Igor would come to exercise more and more influence over its trade agreements, since anyone signing a contract with Jack would want to make sure the pact wasn't nullified should Lindelor's prince meet an untimely end.

In addition, the Zakovian prince would use every bit of influence and pressure to leverage money out of Lindelor. The principality's citizens, now so happy in their idyllic way of life, would come to live under a cloud.

Kim must be persuaded to honor their agreement. And Jack had to keep her safe. But he couldn't very well ignore the invitation when it was known that he was in town. To do so would be to commit a diplomatic breach.

Hearing a noise behind him, he turned and stepped inside as Kim wandered out of the bedroom. Blinking against the sunshine, she regarded him quizzically, her expression sleep soft and open.

Reddish gold hair curled around her face, and the bright light glinted off her deep green eyes. In her red-and-white striped sleep shirt, she resembled an overgrown pixie.

Overgrown in all the right places, Jack noted as she stretched, molding the T-shirt to her breasts. How was he going to endure another night in her bedroom, unable to touch or hold her?

At least Siegfried had gone out this morning and purchased a pair of twin beds to replace that sagging excuse for a double. He'd also bought crisp new curtains, a comfortable sofa and Persian carpets to cover key regions of worn shag.

Other than quizzing him to make sure the Persian carpets hadn't been manufactured by child labor, Kim hadn't said much. It was as if she no longer felt attached to her old possessions.

She was still confused and disoriented. If he had been a more predatory man, Jack felt sure he could use those circumstances to manipulate her into doing what he wished. But even if it hadn't gone against his ethics, he didn't want Kim to end up hating him.

"How do you feel?" he asked, deliberately making no move to approach her.

"Better," she admitted.

"Hans said you had a long talk with your aunt." Jack would have given a great deal to know what the topic had been.

"Did he also mention that he asked her out on a date?"

The comment was so unexpected, it took Jack a moment to react. In the ten years since Hans's divorce, the foreign minister had shown little interest in women. The man expended most of his time and energy on work. "He did?"

"They seem to like each other." Kim ran her fingers through her hair, fluffing and clumping it at the same time. Now she resembled a pixie who'd been caught in a windstorm. "They're a good match, in a funny way."

"Did he discuss anything about our country?"

"You mean did he mention my duty? About a dozen times." She was obviously exaggerating. Surely Hans was more diplomatic than that. Jack only wished his minister's nagging had done some good.

Perhaps the Zakovian ball would help Kim understand his people's plight. The woman was a sharp enough observer to see the rapacious nature beneath Igor's civility.

He fought down his reluctance to bring her into the presence of his enemy. There would be no immediate danger, after all.

"Tomorrow, I would appreciate it if you would accompany me to a diplomatic event," he said.

"Event?" Stifling another yawn, Kim padded ahead of him to the kitchen, where she poured herself a cup of coffee. Siegfried had gone out while she was sleeping to shop for new sheets and towels.

Jack explained about the ball. "It's in the afternoon, which is the custom in our part of the world."

Emerald eyes regarded him over the gold-leafed

rim of the cup. "A ball? Jack, I haven't got anything remotely appropriate to wear."

"Siggy will manage," he said. "Just let him take your measurements and he can go find something tonight while we're dining with your parents."

She snapped the cup down into its saucer. "I most certainly will not! I don't let strange men handle my body, even ones who cook like angels."

"Haven't you ever had anything tailor-made?" Jack dismissed her baggy shirt with a shake of the head. "I mean real clothes?"

"I buy real clothes off the rack, thank you," said his wife. "Most of us weren't born with silver spoons in our mouths. Just tell him I'm a size nine."

Come to think of it, even Kim's wedding dress had been purchased at a bridal boutique, Jack recalled. Apparently it, like everything else in America, came prepackaged. But Kim had tried on quite a few before making her selection, and there was no time for that now.

He couldn't let his wife show up at a Zakovian formal ball wearing an ill-fitting gown. It would reflect poorly on his country, and Jack would never do anything to embarrass the citizens of Lindelor.

"If I understand correctly, the sizes aren't all that standardized," he pointed out. "Siggy can't bring an entire boutique back here for you to try on, and I doubt there'll be many shops open on a Sunday morning. If you won't let him touch you, I'll take your measurements."

Her annoyance vanished in a fit of giggles. "You? The prince of Lindelor is going to make like a tailor?"

Jack drew himself up. "I've had it done to me a thousand times. It can't be that difficult."

"You wouldn't know where to begin!" Kim challenged.

He couldn't back down now. "I think I might have some idea." Ducking into the living room, Jack found his valet's sewing kit and pulled out a tape measure. He felt rather proud of himself until Kim pointed out that it was marked in centimeters.

"I don't know if it will make any difference, but it might." Finishing her coffee, she proceeded to the bedroom, where she fished a tape measure from the mess in one of her drawers. "That's more like it. Inches and feet."

"Very well." Jack located a pad and paper on the bedside table. "Now take off your clothes."

Merriment danced in her eyes. "Excuse me?"

"I can hardly measure you through that shirt!" He heaved an exasperated breath. "Put on a bathing suit, if you insist."

She closed the bedroom door. "Nonsense. I'm game if you are."

"I told you, I can do a perfectly decent job of taking your measure. We'll keep this strictly impersonal."

Jack took pride in his ability to handle every detail not only of Lindelor's business interests but also, if necessary, of his own personal life. He could cook an omelet, run a vacuum cleaner and had once ironed a shirt. In the face of those tasks, a low-tech measuring tape should be easy to manage.

"Go to it," said Kim, and pulled the T-shirt over her head.

THE IDEA OF HAVING JACK take her dimensions had seemed amusing, but as soon as he wrapped the tape around her bare waist, Kim discovered that she'd made a mistake.

She was almost painfully aware of the way his strong hands brushed against her skin. When he moved down to check her hips, ripples of fire ran through her.

From the way his breathing raced, she could tell he was affected too. But since they'd started, they might as well get it over with.

Trying to distract herself by thinking about how she was going to call the financial adviser on Monday didn't help either. Not when Jack was tracing the length of one leg from hip to ankle, his palms firm against her flesh.

Soon he would be leaving. What a relief that would be, except that judging by the way she felt right now, his fingerprints would be permanently burned into her thigh.

"Done?" she asked.

"Do try to develop a little patience." He jotted down his findings.

"You seem to be doing a good job," she said. "Maybe you missed your true calling."

A darkly masculine smile quirked at her as the prince straightened. "Indeed?"

If he *had* been a ladies' tailor in some former life, Kim felt certain his clients would have done their utmost to seduce him in the back room. Had she met him under different circumstances, she supposed she might have had similar inclinations.

She'd certainly never met an American man with such instinctively regal bearing. Jack looked like a prince even while performing a mundane task. Well, it couldn't exactly be called mundane, not when he was standing behind her, positioning the tape around her breasts.

To Kim's embarrassment, her nipples tightened. She was almost certain he would notice through the thin fabric of her bra. "Surely you don't need to..."

"I insist on doing this properly." He spoke near her ear, his lips unexpectedly close.

Her eyelids fluttered shut. Struggle as she might to restrain herself, her head leaned back of its own accord, finding support in the curve of his shoulder.

The tape dropped away as his hands cupped her breasts, sending exquisite agony through her body. A sigh issued from deep inside Kim.

From behind, Jack's mouth traced her neck as he pulled her against him. His hard masculine response branded her soft bottom, and Kim felt her resistance melting.

He turned her, claiming her mouth before she could protest. One of his hands caught her shoulder and the other touched her hip, his movements almost boyishly awkward.

He lifted his head and their green gazes interlocked. In his face, she saw an unguarded tenderness that had never been there before.

"Jack?" she whispered.

He drew back. "I'm sorry, I didn't do a very good job of getting that last measurement."

"Who cares?"

His chuckle broke the tension. "Who cares, indeed? But we aren't really free to do as we choose, are we?"

"It depends on whether we're prepared to take the

consequences.'' Kim tried to slow the urgency of her breathing. "I thought those consequences—a baby— were what you wanted.''

"Then you've changed your mind?''

"No,'' she admitted.

With a sigh, Jack handed her the tape. "I believe you had better take that measurement yourself.''

"But it won't be nearly as much fun.'' However, she complied and gave him the number to write down. "And don't you need my shoulder-to-waist measurement? I don't think I could manage that.''

"If you've never done this before, how do you know what I need?'' he accused as he took the tape, stood behind her and performed the calculation at arm's length.

"I took a sewing class once in high school,'' she said.

"A woman of many talents.''

"Have you ever seen a blouse where the buttons miss the buttonholes by half an inch?'' she demanded. "And one sleeve is shorter than the other? I sew like I sing—off-key.''

"I do hope you dance slightly better than that,'' he said. "We shall be expected to do so tomorrow.''

"Just promise we won't have to perform that Cinderella-and-the-prince number where we waltz around the room while everyone watches,'' Kim said.

"Only when we give our own ball in Lindelor.''

And that, she thought with a trace of sadness, would never happen. "All right, I'll dance. If Siegfried can find me a dress that remotely fits.''

"He'll do better than that,'' Jack promised.

KIM STARED AT HERSELF in the mirror. She had never seen fabric like this, a sophisticated blend of amber tones glimmering with golden highlights that made her hair shine and her eyes appear luminous.

Beneath the low-cut neck, her breasts revealed more cleavage than Kim had thought she possessed. Diaphanous sleeves, a fitted waist and a gossamer skirt with a scarf hemline transformed her into an enigmatic creature, both romantic and seductive.

It was a dangerous dress. Siegfried had brought no others, only this, as if having discerned from the moment he saw it that nothing else would do.

He'd thought of every other detail as well, from high-heeled shoes to a hairdresser and makeup artist who had arrived this morning. Now the last trace of Kim's bruises had vanished beneath ivory foundation, while a delicate diamond tiara shone in the red-gold upsweep of her hair.

It was a good thing Siegfried came prepared, because Kim had forgotten all about the ball by the time she and Jack returned from her parents' house the night before. Her thoughts had been too busy tracking the undercurrents beneath the chatter about Tim's children and her mother's gardening club.

When he wasn't paying attention, her father's face settled into a worried frown. If Kim had arranged an investment in his business, the news obviously hadn't reached him.

After returning home she'd fallen instantly asleep in her new twin bed, only to awaken in the early hours, every sense alert to Jack's even breathing and potent nearness. Her breasts relived his caress, and she could still feel his masculine imprint on her derriere. She ached for him through uncounted chunks of time until exhaustion claimed her again.

This morning she'd awakened in her redecorated apartment and relished the bright pattern of the curtains and the crispness of new sheets. It surprised her a little that she felt no disorientation at the vast changes Siegfried had made, only a mild sense of relief.

There'd been no nostalgia for the old furnishings gleaned from friends and garage sales in her younger days. The lingering effects of amnesia apparently included putting a distance between her present and former selves. Sometimes, even with most memories restored, Kim no longer felt quite certain who she was.

That fact made it all the more unsettling to see herself transformed into a more sophisticated woman. And today she would be surrounded by people who viewed her not as Kim Norris, real-estate title rep, but as the Princess of Lindelor.

What if—scary thought—that was really who she was meant to be?

She shook her head at her reflection. She must not allow herself to fantasize.

Jack hadn't asked her to be his life companion, only the mother of his child. Her choice was either to accept their temporary liaison or to end it.

Tomorrow. Tomorrow she would find out what had happened to the money.

A sharp rap at the door announced that Jack, too, was ready. Taking a deep breath, Kim called, "Come in!"

Opening it, he stood backlit by a wash of early afternoon sunshine. It intensified the scarlet perfection of his jacket and framed a body of unsurpassed height and proportion.

Kim had departed the previous day before Jack

donned the traditional uniform of the Prince of Lindelor. Although she'd seen the gold-braided coat and ebony pants hanging from a rack, she couldn't have imagined the aura of grandeur it acquired when draped over Jack's splendid form.

He looked untouchable and remote, with his head held high and his body almost arrogant in its lordly stance. But there was nothing cold about the way he was staring at her.

"You really are a princess," he murmured.

Before the intensity of his gaze, Kim took an instinctive step backward, which made her wobble slightly on her new heels. "It's all done with smoke and mirrors."

Jack gave a brief nod, as if acknowledging that he'd overstepped his bounds. "The compliment was well meant but perhaps inappropriate. I'm not trying to turn you into something you're not."

Reluctantly, Kim conceded the point. "Some things have to be born inside us or they can never be real."

He offered her a scarlet-sleeved arm, and gingerly she took it.

"Our carriage awaits," said the prince. "In a manner of speaking."

Chapter Seven

Jack handed Kim out of the Rolls-Royce in front of the Luxe Regency Hotel, a massive rococo structure that had been refurbished to the elegance of its 1920s heyday. In her gown and tiara, she was a vision from a fairy tale.

Passersby and the homeless paused on the sidewalk, drinking in the sight of her. Had he not been so alert to any possible danger, Jack wouldn't have been able to take his eyes off her, either.

Kim had attracted him from the moment they met, with her lively intelligence and innate sensuality. But the way she looked tonight revealed an elegance and dignity he hadn't noticed before.

Although not tall, she dominated the space through which she moved. Without speaking, she became the automatic focus of attention.

With a sigh, Jack offered his arm and escorted his wife into the velvet-draped lobby. He wished they were going somewhere other than a Zakovian ball.

Their small entourage, which consisted of Ladislaw and Pierre, followed at a discreet distance. Hans had promised to meet them here.

A notice board pointed the way to the ballroom.

As they passed through hushed hallways, a number of formally dressed men and women turned to watch. This time, the attention contained not only curiosity but calculation. These were Zakovian nobles, who stood to lose or profit depending on the future of Jack's marriage.

He stiffened and brought his emotions under tight rein. Since childhood, he had been forced to master the art of discretion. He would show these people no sign of his anxiety.

"I hope I remember everything you told me." Kim's voice provided a welcome distraction. She had been briefed that morning on when and how to curtsy.

"I should have taught you court etiquette earlier, but I didn't expect you to need it." Jack laid his hand over hers. "Everyone knows you're American, so I'm sure they'll forgive any lapses."

"But I won't," she said with a note of determination that reminded him of his own approach to duty.

Outside the ballroom, a pair of guards glanced at Jack and ushered the Lindelorians inside with the faintest of nods. From the bulges beneath their coats, he could see that security was tight.

Not that Prince Igor had anything to fear, but the man was paranoid about safety. Jack had read once that people tended to project their own motivations and characteristics onto others. So the would-be assassin naturally feared being assassinated himself.

He glanced at Kim, but she was taking in the assemblage wide-eyed. This whole world of political infighting was completely foreign to her.

He hoped he could keep it that way.

AN ARRAY OF POTTED greenery transformed the ballroom into a garden, giving Kim the sensation that she was stepping into another world. Roses on a trellis perfumed the air, with dwarf orange and lemon trees adding their own rich scents.

On a platform sat a small orchestra, playing a waltz. Above them, on a second platform, stood a purple-draped throne.

At floor level circulated lords and ladies, or at least she assumed that's what they were. The gowns ranged from stiff and jewel-encrusted to frothy designer concoctions, while the men wore a rainbow of tuxedos and uniforms.

On either side of the room, small tables had been set up with tiers of delicacies and fountains of champagne. Since it was midafternoon, Kim assumed that either most of these people had breakfasted late or that the food was simply part of the show.

"I thought Zakovia had financial problems." She stood on tiptoe to speak close to Jack's ear. The nearness brought a temptation to nuzzle him, which she resisted.

"It does. Severe ones." He inclined his head formally, not looking directly at her. "But Prince Igor spares himself and his guests no luxury."

"Why?"

Jack nodded to a middle-aged couple, who curtsied and bowed as they passed. "Igor believes it is his country's duty to indulge him."

"Surely all this money would be better invested in economic development!"

"Indeed it would." Jack bowed to an open-faced young man in a black-trimmed gray uniform, who stood halfway across the room. The man's face brightened as he spotted them. "I'm surprised to see him here."

"Is he a friend?" she asked as the man strode toward them, smiling.

"Not exactly. I don't know him all that well," Jack said. "He's the Grand Duke Kristoffer, Prince Igor's son. He's a competitive diver. As a matter of fact, he went to college in England with Angela. She thinks highly of him."

"Prince Jacques!" Reaching them, Kristoffer shook hands vigorously. "I'm so glad you could come. We were all worried when we heard about your wife's accident."

"Princess Kimberly, may I present the Grand Duke Kristoffer," Jack said.

"Oh, let's not be so formal." The grand duke bowed. "Call me Kris, will you?"

"With pleasure," she said, making a slight curtsy. She liked this man instantly. In his early twenties, he apparently belonged to a different era and a different mentality than his father.

His next question surprised her. "Has Angela arrived?"

"Angela?" Jack frowned. "What on earth would she be doing here?"

"She's en route to a medical trade show in Hawaii. As a matter of fact, she said she was filling in for you." The slender blond man studied the crowd. "There she is! Excuse me. A pleasure meeting you, Princess." With another bow, off he loped toward someone Kim couldn't see in the press of guests.

Jack frowned. "I'd forgotten. I did ask her to attend for me. But how did Kristoffer know she'd be stopping in Los Angeles, when I didn't?"

"Obviously, she told him," Kim pointed out. She wished the prince would relax and enjoy himself. He was taking this ball much too seriously. Weren't people supposed to have fun? And did his aides have to pace around the room as if guarding against imminent danger?

Then she saw his private secretary, Pierre, gazing with fascination at Kristoffer. It took only an instant to ascertain that the object of his interest was not the grand duke but the young lady at his side.

"I think your assistant likes Angela," Kim murmured.

"Excuse me?" The furrow on Jack's brow deepened. "Good heavens, he's certainly ogling her, isn't he? Well, Angela's broken her share of hearts, I should think."

Now that the crowd had parted a little, Kim could see why. Kristoffer had slipped his arm around the waist of a tall young woman with raven-dark hair, animated features and a merry smile.

"They're awfully chummy," Jack grumbled.

"It could be a good thing, couldn't it?" she asked. "If they were to marry, Lindelor's future would be in good hands."

"Only if I outlive Prince Igor," he said. "I'm twenty years his junior, but his family is very long-lived. A decade or so in his hands and our economy would be gutted. Maybe even faster than that." He glanced around, his expression wary, and Kim realized it could be awkward if his comments were overheard. "Shall we dance?"

"I thought you'd never ask." She had to repress a tendency to skip as they headed for the dance floor, where the orchestra was playing another waltz.

The guests made way for them. Kim felt a trifle self-conscious as Jack placed one hand formally on her waist and took her hand in his. With so many people observing, she was grateful he kept a formal distance between them.

Then the music caught hold of her and she began to sway in Jack's arms. Despite their decorous movements, she could read every twinge of his response to her in the sudden tightening of his arms and the muscle that jumped in his jaw. His heat enveloped her, melding them into a single life-form as they stepped out in instinctive unison.

Around them, the dancers twirled in a pattern far more organized than anything she'd expected, but Jack guided her smoothly. They circled with a heady speed that sent Kim's scarf-hemmed skirt floating out, carving designs in the air.

The voices of onlookers reached her as she and Jack whirled by, and to her surprise she was able to pick out a few comments. "She's nice-enough looking, for an American.... Rather a showy dress, don't you think...? Why do you suppose she accepted him? It must be for his money."

The cattiness bothered her until Kim remembered that these were Zakovians, who had a personal stake in not wanting Lindelor to produce an heir. Still, she wished they could be more charitable.

"Don't let these aristocrats bother you." Jack's voice was low and gentle. "The common people of both countries are the salt of the earth. And the nobles at my court are considerably more kindhearted."

"I'm sure they are." *And I'm not going to be married to you long enough to find out, anyway.* Kim didn't know whether the thought relieved or saddened her.

Her attention was happily diverted by a new couple on the dance floor, Kristoffer and Angela. The two had a comfortable way of moving that indicated this wasn't the first time they'd danced together.

Apparently this relationship was more advanced than Jack realized. Kim wondered whether the still absent Prince Igor approved.

The music segued into a new tune. Pierre, a hank of blond hair draped defiantly over his forehead, appeared at Angela's elbow. "You did promise me a dance the next time we met, my lady," he said.

The grand duke regarded the interloper speculatively, then stepped aside with a gallant bow. Angela turned to her new partner with a slightly forced smile.

She warmed again as they neared Kim and Jack. "Hullo, Princess Kimberly! I'm your cousin, Angela Schnappsenfeld! Sorry we haven't been formally introduced."

His hand firm on Kim's waist, the prince maintained their position adjacent to the other couple. "I'll be pleased to remedy that, Lady Angela."

"It's not necessary!" chirped the tall woman, her hair rioting as Pierre spun her around. "I do love American manners! We just say hello, and we're old chums!"

The couple flashed away, leaving Kim to ponder the fact that Angela didn't look at all the worse for wear now that she had recovered from her motorcycle accident. Apparently the woman's internal injuries hadn't affected her in any visible way.

Before she could query Jack further, the music

stopped and the lights went out. Since the ballroom had no windows, the room plunged into darkness.

"Blackout?" Kim asked in surprise.

"Theatrics," muttered her husband.

His comment was borne out a moment later by a drumroll, followed by a pair of spotlights flashing across the throne. No longer empty, it was now occupied by a king, or at least Kim would have believed him to be one had she not known that his title was Prince Igor.

He was a man of medium height and coloring, with a squarish face and a cruel scar blazing across one cheek. On his head sat a crown, glimmering with jewels.

A long purple cape fell from his shoulders into arranged folds. Beneath it, he wore a gray velvet uniform like his son's, except that instead of shoes he had chosen knee-high black boots.

"The Tsar of All the Russias," whispered Kim, and heard Jack choke back laughter beside her.

Prince Igor raised his arms. "Welcome!" His voice bore a slight accent. "We are pleased to have such distinguished guests today! Please enjoy yourselves!" It sounded like a command rather than an invitation.

If we don't enjoy ourselves, will he cut off our heads? Kim wondered.

Mercifully, the lights came up, and the orchestra launched into a militaristic theme. Prince Igor paced down from his throne, accompanied by a small knot of fawning courtiers.

He headed for Jack, and the two men gave each other low bows. Kim sank into a curtsy, wishing she had had a chance to practice more and hoping her knees wouldn't crack.

When she stood up, the Prince of Zakovia took her hand and kissed it drily. "It is a pleasure to meet my new neighbor." He radiated a watchful coldness that reminded Kim of a cat stalking a bird.

"I was surprised to see Grand Duke Kristoffer here," Jack told the Zakovian ruler.

"Ah! He attends an international swim competition in—how do you pronounce it?—Mission Viejo." Igor got the Spanish pronunciation—Vee-AY-ho—exactly right. This was not a man who left anything to chance.

Instinctively, Kim's gaze sought the young man in the gray uniform. She spotted him talking to Angela and Pierre. Just behind them, she glimpsed a tall blond woman, partially obscured.

There was something familiar about the woman, but Kim couldn't place her. It was almost as if she were seeing a figment from a dream.

"Jack?" she said. "Do you know who—"

"Well, well." He chuckled. "Look at Hans!"

Their entire party, Prince Igor included, swiveled toward the dance floor to take in the sight of the lean foreign minister executing a stunning tango with Valerie Norris.

They stalked each other across the dance floor, tigress and tiger in turn. Then Hans swept his partner into his arms so dramatically that wisps of brown hair flew loose from her French twist. It was the first time Kim had ever seen Valerie look anything but bandbox perfect.

"That's my aunt!" she said. "What's she doing here?"

"Obviously, Hans brought her," Jack said.

"Your aunt?" Igor spoke with forced joviality. "I

did not realize the nobility of Lindelor had other female members.''

"She's my father's sister," Kim said. "The other side of the family."

He gave a gracious nod. She wondered if she was imagining the relief in his expression.

A few minutes later, Prince Igor excused himself to welcome the head of the foreign-affairs council, an influential group of business and civic leaders. At his departure, Kim felt the tension seep from her body.

"What did you think of him?" Jack asked quietly.

"He's kind of scary," she admitted. "But then, I don't know many heads of state. None, other than you."

"He *is* scary." Before Jack could elaborate, Hans and Valerie approached, at the same time that Angela and Kristoffer headed their way from the opposite direction.

In the flurry of greetings and introductions that followed, Kim forgot whatever questions had been nagging at the back of her mind. She was too interested in observing the fond looks between her aunt and the foreign minister and the way Kristoffer couldn't seem to stop touching Angela.

"He helped me with my physical therapy after the crash," the Lindelorian woman explained. "The doctor recommended a lot of swimming. You should see him dive, Kim! He's going to win an Olympic medal someday."

Jack didn't seem to object to their friendship, and Kim found herself somewhat relieved about the future of Lindelor and Zakovia. Kristoffer appeared to be a different sort of man from his father. The possibility that he rather than Igor might someday rule Lindelor somewhat relieved her sense of guilt at the prospect of ending her marriage.

Oddly, though, attending the ball had proved more pleasant than she had expected. Kim actually enjoyed the formality, and it was fun meeting a new cousin. It was tempting to think about visiting Lindelor, just for a little while, just to meet other relatives and see the sights her grandfather had described so lovingly, if Jack wouldn't mind.

Kim bit her lip. Why was she toying with the idea of delaying her divorce? Did it have anything to do with the electricity that had surged through her when Jack put his hand on her waist and they danced together?

She must not yield to a misguided infatuation. The terms of their marriage had been quite clear and quite temporary. It was urgent that she call a halt before they ignited a blaze she couldn't handle.

AFTER THE BALL, Jack invited his cousin and Kristoffer, Hans and Valerie and the two aides to join them for dinner. Kim suggested Chinatown, a few blocks to the north, and everyone agreed.

A short time later, sitting among the happily chattering couples beneath a paper lantern, Jack felt old and cynical by comparison, even though he was at least ten years younger than his foreign minister.

The day weighed on his mind with its undercurrent of danger. Most of all, his gut twisted every time he thought about the way Kim was single-mindedly pursuing a divorce.

Hardly tasting his *kung pao* shrimp and lemon chicken, he drank in her nearness. Sitting beside him, savoring every bite of food and every morsel of conversation, she bloomed like an alpine spring. He couldn't separate the appeal of her satiny skin and tantalizing cleavage from the yearning he felt to hear her thoughts and share her enthusiasms.

It was immature, he knew, to indulge himself in such passionate sentimentality. Kim was the only means of saving his country from a perilous future. Jack's sense of honor allowed him to influence her for altruistic reasons, but not to manipulate her for his own satisfaction.

By not doing his utmost to help her end the marriage, he was subjecting her to deadly danger. Were his motives really unselfish? How could he be sure he was only thinking of his country, when every whiff of her perfume made him ache to possess her?

He must make sure he was charting this course for the good of Lindelor, and not because his body grew hard and hungry whenever she came near. He knew his duty. What he did not know and could not allow himself to consider, was the depth of his own feelings.

ON MONDAY MORNING, Kim called the financial adviser and asked whether she had recently invested a large sum of money.

She heard computer keys clicking on the other end of the line as he checked his records. "No, it looks like I haven't received anything from you for a few months."

Her heart sank. She'd been counting on locating the money swiftly. "I didn't even discuss making a large investment?"

"I don't believe so," he said. "In the past few weeks? Definitely not."

After the exhilarating events of the day before, attending the ball, seeing her aunt in Hans's arms and meeting Kristoffer and Angela, Kim had awakened in a good mood. It was rapidly evaporating.

"I can't imagine where I put it." She explained about the amnesia. "Everything's coming back, except for a few gaps here and there. Unfortunately, this is one of them."

"My guess would be that you stashed the money in a savings account," the adviser said. "Just for the short term."

"I hope you're right."

She spent the next hour calling every financial institution in the area. What she learned was that she had no accounts except the ones she already knew about. And the amounts in them tallied with the totals in her records.

Her hopes rose when she rummaged through her drawers again and discovered the key to a safe-deposit box. But when she visited the bank, all she found inside were the pink slip to her car, a passport she'd acquired two years ago before a vacation trip to Australia and a few other documents.

Since Jack was tied up this morning, Pierre had accompanied Kim to the bank. The young man walked her inside and waited in the lobby.

"You don't have to do this, you know," she said as she came out. "I'm probably going to spend the rest of the morning touching base with clients, and then I've got a doctor's appointment. You'll be bored silly."

"It's more interesting than answering telephone calls," the assistant said as he held the car door for her. "Your Highness, is anything wrong? You look upset."

"Well, how would you feel if you lost a million dollars?" she asked.

Pierre slid into the passenger seat, since Kim had insisted on driving. "Lost it?"

"I want to pay Jack back so we can get a divorce," she said. "Didn't he tell you?"

The assistant shook his head. "That's rather hard for Lindelor, isn't it?"

"I'm sorry about that." Putting the car in gear, Kim backed out of the parking space. "Maybe we could arrange an egg donation—no, I couldn't do that either. I want old-fashioned things like a home and raising my own children."

"And you couldn't do that in Lindelor?" queried her companion.

She could hardly explain that Jack hadn't asked her to. Besides, she doubted this fiery attraction between them would last, given their deep-rooted differences. "It isn't that simple."

"I'm sure the money will turn up." Pierre gave her a friendly smile. "After all, the amnesia seems to be nearly gone. Have you recalled anything about your accident?"

Pausing at a signal to turn onto Coast Highway, Kim felt her body grow cold. For no discernible reason, her breath caught in her throat and her hands began to perspire. "No. It—it frightens me for some reason. I don't even want to think about it."

"Forgive me." The blond man shook his head apologetically. "I'm overstepping myself. I suppose I'm a bit distracted this morning."

"Because of Angela?" Kim guessed as she headed north toward a real-estate office where she transacted a lot of business.

He gave her a startled look. "Is it that obvious?"

"You asked her to dance," Kim pointed out.

"We're old friends," he said. "All right, I'd like us to be more than that. I don't have much to offer compared to a grand duke, but I do hope to hold a position of importance someday. And I suspect Kristoffer's affections will be transitory. He's known as a ladies' man."

"Poor Angela," said Kim. "But for your sake, I hope you're right."

She spent the rest of the morning touching base with real-estate agents. Pierre proved a pleasant companion on the drive between offices and talking to him soothed Kim's nerves.

As they headed home for lunch before her doctor's appointment, she felt herself tensing again. Even though her business was going well, she would never be able to repay the million dollars out of her commissions.

One way or another, she was going to have to find a way to satisfy Prince Jack.

Chapter Eight

Jack had barely been able to concentrate all morning, during a meeting with a potential new trading partner from Mexico. He kept thinking about the near collision while Hans was driving on Saturday, and the relief on Igor's face when he learned that Valerie—not quite past her childbearing years—wasn't descended from Lindelorian nobility.

Danger might threaten Kim at any moment. He had to take her to safety until either their child was born or they were divorced.

Pierre had been alerted to the danger, of course. A young man with quick reflexes, he should prove at least as good a protector as Hans. But Jack couldn't help worrying.

It was a relief to see Kim at her apartment, where they shared a lunch of chicken salad and lemon-poppy seed muffins. Pierre, downcast to learn that Angela had already flown to Hawaii, declined their invitation to stay, and Siegfried retreated diplomatically into the living room.

"I couldn't find the money," Kim admitted when they were alone. "But the way my memory is returning, I'm sure it will come back to me soon."

Jack wondered, not for the first time, what she'd needed it for. As a nest egg, or for some specific project? But if she didn't wish to volunteer the information, he had no intention of prying.

"Unfortunately, I'm not going to be able to stay in America much longer." He touched his cloth napkin to the corners of his mouth. "In another week, my country is hosting a major swimming-and-diving competition. It is important to our prestige that I should be there."

"You're going back to Lindelor?" Kim stared at him with frank disappointment. "Already?"

"In a few days." But not while she was in danger, he thought grimly. He wanted to ask her to come with him, but such a request was likely to precipitate an immediate demand for an end of the marriage. "Let's see what your doctor has to say. Maybe he'll have some suggestions about recovering the rest of your memory."

She nodded. "I suppose...but, Jack..."

"Hmm?"

"It's just that we seem to be having fun," she admitted. "I'd hate for it to end so soon."

The statement gave him pause. Fun was not something Jack was used to, having grown up with an ailing father and the knowledge that he might have to assume the throne at any time. Yet he *had* enjoyed the ball, despite his worries.

That night he'd lain awake for a long time, wishing Siegfried had bought a single large bed instead of two small ones. He wanted to feel Kim roll against him, to touch her back and smell her hair. Even if they didn't make love, he wanted to hold her close.

He didn't see how he could leave, under the circumstances. But he had already been away from Lindelor too long.

Kim regarded him thoughtfully. "I wish things were different between us, that we'd met in the normal way. But of course, we couldn't have, could we? Princes and title reps don't usually trip over each other."

"What about taking your friend up on his idea?" he asked. "We could steal a few days by ourselves in the mountains before I leave. I enjoy skiing, and you did say you wanted to learn."

Wariness replaced her open expression. "You wouldn't have an ulterior motive, by chance?"

He could hardly admit that his goal was to whisk her away from danger. Besides, he *did* want more than that, much more. If he could persuade her to change her mind about the baby, there would be nothing unethical about that.

"I'd like to give you a chance to reconsider," Jack conceded. "After all, you were willing to have my child before the accident. Perhaps when your memory fully returns, you'll feel that way again."

Emotions warred in her eyes. How easy it was to read her feelings, he thought, and how endearing that trait was. She wanted him just as he wanted her, but she, too, held herself in check. "I could never give up our baby."

"You wouldn't have to," he reminded her. "You could visit. When the child is older, it could spend some vacation time with you."

"From a royal palace to a tiny apartment?" Kim murmured. "What a shock to the system."

"From the frozen Alps to sunny California?" he countered. "Every youngster's dream."

She laughed. "You're very persuasive, but I don't think…"

"I'll leave Siggy at home," he promised. "You may be surprised to learn that I can live like any normal person."

"It would almost be worth the trip, just to see you try to whip up a meal." She cocked her head at him. "The prince and the pepper. But hey, it's time to leave for my doctor's appointment. I have to stop at one real-estate office en route, but that shouldn't take more than half an hour."

"No problem." That was when the idea struck him. It was a bit high-handed, but Jack had only a few days left before duty called him home. "I just have to make one phone call first."

THE DOCTOR, WHOSE office was located adjacent to the hospital, announced himself pleased with Kim's recovery. Her reflexes were normal, and since a CT scan at the hospital had shown no serious damage, he predicted a full return of her memory.

"Except possibly for the moments before the injury itself," he cautioned. "Unfortunately, trauma victims sometimes never get that sort of thing back. It's more a psychological than a physiological block, we suspect."

"Can I resume exercising?" Kim asked.

"A moderate amount shouldn't hurt," the doctor said. "Nothing that could get you bopped on the head, though."

"No trampolining, I promise," she said.

"Congratulations," Jack offered as they rode down the elevator. "It looks like you're on the road to recovery."

"Actually, I feel like I've already recovered," Kim admitted. "I seem to have a lot of pent-up energy."

"Good," he said.

She was about to ask him why, when they stepped out of the medical building. As she blinked against the bright sunshine, Kim experienced a sense of dislocation that was becoming all too common.

It was as if she recognized where she was, but felt no connection to it. In the past, she had looked forward to her daily life: making contact with clients, picking up dinner at a favorite restaurant, reading in her apartment, jogging on the beach.

Today she felt as if she'd seen those things in a movie. Now her sharpest memories were of the Zakovian ball and sharing coffee with Jack at the bakery and eating Siegfried's fabulous cooking.

Instinctively, she placed her hand on Jack's arm, as if he were her only link with reality.

"Dizzy?" he asked with concern.

"Just not quite myself." That was as close as she could come to summing up this odd sensation. Was it due to the head injury or to worry over the missing money or to her feelings about Jack?

If it was the latter, Kim hoped this confusion would pass. One way or the other, he would soon be leaving her world and returning to his own. She needed to get back to normal.

She felt even more dazed as Jack escorted her to the car. Another sedan like the ones rented by the Lindelorian staff was pulling away, and she could have sworn she recognized the man at the wheel.

"Is that Siegfried?" she asked in confusion.

"Apparently so," Jack murmured as he helped her into her seat.

"What was he doing here?"

"Just putting a few things in the trunk. You'll see why in a few minutes." With a teasing grin, he backed out of the space and headed down from the hillside medical complex.

The long driveway ran along a sea cliff, with a sheer drop on one side. Near a curve, a panel truck blocked one lane while a red-haired man replaced a tire. As they slowed, Jack peered out warily.

"What's wrong?"

"It's dangerous, the way he's narrowed the road, especially next to a cliff." He halted the car about fifty feet short of the curve.

The red-haired man lifted his head and stared at them in exasperation. Impatiently, he gestured to them to proceed.

"There's nobody else around," Kim pointed out. "Go ahead."

"Just a minute." The prince tapped his fingers against the steering wheel, watching the man lift a tire into place.

Behind them, Kim heard a siren. Turning, she spotted a flashing red light heading from the hospital. "It's an ambulance. We've got to move."

Without a word, Jack put the car into gear and sped past the truck. A moment later, the ambulance took the same course, then flashed around them.

"What was that all about?" Kim asked as they reached the highway.

"Just being cautious," said the prince.

"Are you in some kind of danger?" Now that she thought about it, Kim wondered why the possibility hadn't occurred to her before. "Is Prince Igor after you?"

He shook his head tightly. "No."

"How can you be sure?" Kim pressed. "He certainly has a lot to gain."

"Believe me, I'm sure." Jack passed her street, continuing toward downtown Laguna Beach.

"Hey, you—"

"We're not going home." He slowed for pedestrians, then turned right and headed for the freeway.

"It can't be another ball," she said. "Are we having lunch with someone? I know, a picnic! That's what Siegfried was putting in the trunk!"

"Wrong. You get two more guesses." Jack hummed to himself as they sped through Laguna Canyon.

"What else could he have put in there?" Kim tried to picture what the valet might have tucked into the trunk. The only thing that came to mind was suitcases. But why would they need them unless they were going somewhere....

"You scoundrel!" She tried to glare at him but couldn't muster the anger. "You're kidnapping me to that cabin!"

One eyebrow arched. "Do you object? Siggy picked up the key from your boss and packed our clothes, so why not?"

"I don't like surprises." Kim hesitated as they approached the freeway. If she protested forcefully, she knew Jack would turn around. And she didn't want him to.

Darn it, if Jack was flying back to Lindelor in a few days, she wanted more time with him now. It was a great chance to learn to ski, too.

Most of all, the mountains would be a perfect place to sort out her thoughts, away from the other people who kept popping in and out of their lives. With a little peace and quiet, Kim might finally come to terms with the disturbing changes that had taken place inside her. Then she would be ready to resume her old life, carefree and unencumbered.

"I take that back," she said. "I'm beginning to like surprises better all the time."

THE CABIN TURNED OUT to be a two-story A-frame that depended for heat on a wood-burning stove. An undersize refrigerator and a wheezing microwave oven were the only concessions to modern technology. There wasn't even a TV set.

Jack was accustomed to a bit more luxury, but this place had one huge advantage: there was no travel agent involved, and hence no computer records that he and Kim were staying here. Only a few of his staff members knew their whereabouts.

That truck near the hospital had probably been a false alarm. He didn't think Prince Igor's goons would do anything to harm him personally and risk losing all claim to Lindelor. Still, he was glad he'd waited on the road, since the presence of the ambulance would have provided witnesses, not to mention emergency help if necessary.

And now he had several days alone with Kim and a clear shot at winning her back to her patriotic duty, he reflected while lugging in their suitcases. What more could a man ask?

As she stowed away the groceries they'd purchased at a small market, Kim looked more like the woman Jack had first met three weeks earlier, healthy and clearheaded. For the first time since her accident, he began to feel optimistic.

"Ready to try the slopes?" he asked.

"Sure." She closed the refrigerator. "What's the first step?"

"Picking our equipment," he said.

True to Alan's word, the cabin's large service porch held a wide selection of skis, bindings, boots and poles. From the variety available, it was obvious that either Alan had acquired extra equipment as a favor to guests or that some of his friends stored their gear here. In any case, although the quality wasn't quite up to Jack's usual standards, he was able to find appropriate sizes and lengths.

In a closet, they located warm jackets and overalls, a necessity since Kim's wardrobe had yielded nothing suitable. A small bureau in the second bedroom was filled with socks, gloves, caps and goggles.

When their selections were complete, Kim eyed the pile of clothing and equipment laid out in the living room. "If it takes this long to get ready, when do you find time to ski?"

"It won't take this long tomorrow," Jack pointed out. "Come on, Princess. Suit up!"

She gave him a delighted grin. "Something about the mountain air brings out the irreverent side of you."

"You mean I'm the only one affected?" An hour spent helping her pull on boots, measure skis and try fittings had left Jack tingling with her nearness. At every step, he'd had to fight the impulse to remove the items, along with a lot more. "You've relaxed since we got here, and I can think of a few ways to make you even more relaxed."

"If we get any more relaxed, we'll never make it to the ski slopes at all," she warned.

"Would you care?"

"Would you?"

They faced each other across the couch, their breath visibly mingling in the chilly air. A shiver ran through Jack, not from the cold but from his own pent-up longings.

His masculine instincts demanded that he take this woman up on her dare. If he hadn't spent a lifetime mastering self-control, that was exactly what he would have done.

But until she agreed to have his child, the results of such a precipitous union could prove disastrous. Even if she did become pregnant, what was to prevent a nasty custody battle?

Most of all, neither Jack's honor nor his growing sense of closeness to Kim would allow him to take advantage of her. He'd whisked her to the mountains without warning, knowing she was still vulnerable because of her injuries. It was his duty to protect her, even from herself.

"We'd better check out the local resorts while there's still enough daylight." He spoke stiffly, collecting himself with an effort.

Her mouth twisted. "I guess so."

They went out to the car, each lost in thought. The need to pay attention while driving through slushy streets proved a welcome distraction for Jack.

The nearest facility was mercifully uncrowded on a Monday afternoon. There were no classes under way, and he and Kim had the beginner slope virtually to themselves.

"I wish I'd had time to do some exercises," she admitted as she wobbled on her unfamiliar skis. "My muscles aren't in very good shape."

"We won't overdo it," Jack promised. "Now, let me show you how to grasp the poles properly."

While attending college one year in New York, he'd spent his winter vacation as a volunteer instructor for underprivileged children at a ski resort in the Adirondacks. The teaching experience stood him in good stead now, and Kim proved to be an apt pupil.

Showing an instinctive feel for the snow, she quickly mastered the basic position and learned to walk, glide and turn.

Straight schussing proved more of a challenge, and she fell twice before making it down the slope. From the gleam in her eye when she succeeded, Jack could see she was going to enjoy this sport.

With late-afternoon sunlight casting long shadows, he decided to call a halt. If Kim wore herself out today, it would ruin the rest of their visit. Besides, the more tired she became, the greater the risk of falling hard enough to jar her head.

"Mind if I try the advanced slope?" he asked. "I'd like to get the kinks out of my own system."

"Be my guest." Her cheeks red with exertion and her expression vibrant, Kim waved him toward the lift. "I'll find a place to watch."

For a moment, Jack hesitated to leave her. He had sworn to stay close this entire trip, since none of his staff were at hand, but keeping such a tight rein was bound to make her suspicious.

Besides, his entire being cried out for one long, lusty attack on the slope to whip away the demands of his body. And, he admitted ruefully, he did want to show off his skill to his wife.

Taking a careful look around and spotting nothing suspicious, Jack went to ride up the mountain.

KIM COULD FEEL her muscles aching from the workout as she located a bench with a view of the advanced slope. She sank down next to a teenage boy who was listening to a portable CD player on earphones.

Jack had disappeared from sight on the lift. To Kim, the steep slope appeared perilous, pocked with gullies and scrub trees to catch the unwary. Only a few brave souls were daring its rigors today, mostly starting midway and wiping out on the way down.

The boy beside her regarded them with bored indifference, and Kim wondered why he had come until she spotted a middle-aged woman waving to him from the foot of the intermediate slope. The boy shook his head, evidently rejecting his mother's attempt to lure him into exercising.

A few people wandered out of the lodge carrying steaming disposable cups. Hot chocolate or coffee would taste fabulous, Kim thought, but she refused to leave her post until she witnessed Jack's performance.

He had been remarkably patient with her this afternoon. As a beginner, she felt slow and clumsy, but not a single flicker of impatience had crossed his face, even though he must have grown up with people who skied as naturally as others rode bicycles.

Would the man never stop surprising her? Instead of a spoiled playboy, he was turning out to be a keen businessman, principled leader and playful friend.

What kind of lover would he make? A spark of yearning warmed Kim's cheeks, spreading all the way to her marrow.

She could imagine the intense pleasure of every gentle touch as he made love to her, and each deep, commanding thrust. But the true measure of a lover could only be taken afterward, in his steadfastness and loyalty, and those were qualities she had no right to expect. The limits of their relationship had been set, with her own concurrence.

The price, she thought, was too high. If only she had realized that before she accepted the million dollars.

A gasp from the boy beside her dragged Kim out of her reverie. "Wow! Look at that guy! He's all the way up there!"

At the top of the mountain perched a lean figure with royal presence. Prince Jacques stood assessing the course, his expression unreadable behind goggles.

But Kim already knew how his face must look, poised and alert. She thought she could detect a slight anticipatory smile.

Several people stopped to peer upward, forgetting their cups of hot liquid. "Gee, I haven't seen anyone take the whole slope all day," muttered one man.

"Oh, there was one guy," commented his companion, a chunky young woman with dark hair. "He broke his leg."

Great, Kim thought.

Jack pushed off, propelling himself forward and bending into the kind of position she'd seen in Olympic competitions. He picked up speed at a breathtaking rate, zigging and zagging down the mountain face.

"That guy really knows what he's doing," said the teenager, pulling the earphones away from his head as if they interfered with his concentration.

Her heart pounding, Kim could only hope the boy was right. But it was impossible to worry as Jack flashed over the snow, his exhilaration communicated in every flick of the poles and subtle shift of position.

In his movements, she detected an instinctive rhythm, an alpine dance. Man and mountain formed a union that transformed Jack's descent into a kind of lovemaking, as if he were caressing the slope and it was yielding to him.

Only a faint shadow indicated the presence of a gully, but some of the people around Kim had noticed it. "He's going to crash!" said the dark-haired woman. "He's heading right for—"

"I can't look," said another woman.

"He'll make it," the teenager announced confidently.

And he did. The cruel slope must have offered some kind of smooth outcropping, because as Kim watched with grim fascination, the sleek figure became airborne.

Over the gully soared the prince, his blue shadow swooping across the snow beneath him. The two moving shapes rejoined so lightly that Kim wasn't even sure he had landed until she heard applause break out around her.

Jack finished the descent with a dramatic turn that spewed snow into the late-afternoon sunlight, filling the air with glitter. The clapping intensified.

"Fantastic!" The teenager jumped to his feet. "Man, someday I'm going to do that!"

Other viewers called out compliments, and Kim could hear someone asking Jack if he competed on the ski circuit. He extricated himself with a few polite responses and made his way to Kim.

"If you were trying to impress me, you succeeded," she said. "That was terrific!"

"I'll admit, I was showing off." Stepping out of

his skis, Jack grinned with boyish pride. "I suppose it must seem a bit childish."

"You know it wasn't." Without thinking, Kim slipped her arm around his waist. Even through the padded jacket, she could feel his heat. "Everybody enjoyed it."

"Did you?" He bent down and nuzzled her hair, his breath tickling her scalp.

"No. I was bored silly." She ducked away, her eyes daring him to give pursuit, and in a burst of merriment he did.

In their heavy boots, they scrambled across the open space toward the parking lot, dodging between a handful of visitors. In an open field, Jack would have caught her instantly, but here Kim took advantage of every obstacle.

She reached the sedan first, tapping its surface and shouting, "I win! I win!"

He halted a few feet away and surveyed her gleefully. "So you do. But what precisely have you won?"

"A ride home?" she teased.

"And then what?"

"A massage!" It was the first thing that popped into Kim's mind.

Extracting the key from his pocket, Jack unlocked the car. "Very well. A massage it is."

Only as she took her seat inside and felt her breath gradually return to normal did Kim realize that inviting Jack to put his hands all over her body might not have been the wisest decision in the world.

Chapter Nine

They began the evening with dinner, the first they'd cooked together. Baked beans with cut-up hot dogs and canned corn might not be in Siegfried's league, but it tasted delicious eaten in front of a blazing fire.

"Is this what it's like when you go skiing in Lindelor?" Kim asked. "The resort, the cabin, all that sort of thing?"

"Our facilities are a bit more posh." Jack faced the fireplace, one knee up and one leg extended, his back against the couch. "And the mountains are higher."

"That one you took today was high enough." Kim set her plate aside.

He smiled fondly. "Not nearly. You can't get going fast enough unless you've got the distance."

"I think your cousin Angela isn't the only one in the family who's a daredevil," Kim observed. It frightened and yet excited her to picture Jack taking such chances.

He turned to regard her, the firelight casting shadows and gleams across his hair and skin. Highlighted in this way, his cheekbones gave him a faintly exotic air and his green eyes took on smoky depths.

"The LeGrands have always been risk takers," he said. "Nearly sixty years ago, when Zakovia joined the Axis powers, we insisted on neutrality. For a time, it appeared we would be overrun."

"Why weren't you?" Kim asked.

"For one thing, Lindelor was too small and mountainous to be worth expending much trouble on," he conceded. "But more important, as neutrals, we were able to make our medical equipment and medicines available as needed. With bombs destroying so many facilities, both the Allies and the Axis recognized that we were more valuable left alone. But it was a knife-edge we walked."

"I can't imagine how it would feel to know that my family was a part of history." The warmth of the fire, combined with weariness from the day's exertions, made Kim's eyelids droop.

"The LeGrands *are* your family, distantly," the prince reminded her. Setting their dishes aside, he added, "I promised you a back rub. Lie down."

Lacking the energy to argue, Kim stretched out on the rug. It felt soft beneath her sweatshirt and jeans.

A moment later, Jack's large body poised above her and his hands slid up the fabric of her top. Before she could object, he reached down to unsnap her jeans and work them low on her hips.

"I don't think this is a good idea," she murmured, unable to bestir herself. "Maybe we should just go to sleep."

"A promise is a promise." Reaching toward the hearth, he retrieved a small bottle he'd placed there earlier. Kim had assumed it must be a kind of sauce, but now he poured some into his hands and began rubbing it into her back. It felt cool and sleek, and gave off the scent of mountain pine.

"Is that—from Lindelor?" Her head drooped on her arms.

"An herbal lotion." Jack stroked the concoction into her skin. "It's said to heal chapped skin."

He unhooked the back of her bra, letting it fall away as he kneaded her muscles. His hands were powerful but gentle, teasing out knots and finding the sore spots between her shoulder blades.

Instinctively, Kim tensed against the pleasure of the contact, but slowly her resistance melted. What was the harm in relaxing as the warmth of his touch connected itself relay by relay to her private electrical circuit?

When he lowered her jeans farther and thumb-pressed the strain from the small of her back, Kim sank deeper into the spell he was casting. She could smell pine forests and feel the liberating thrill of racing down a mountain. In her mind, castles sprouted on faraway hills and fires crackled on ancient hearths.

Practiced fingers caressed their way up her rib cage and along the sides of her breasts. His palms slipped beneath the soft orbs, cupping her nipples.

Kim felt his mouth graze the center of her back in a series of tingling explorations. As he knelt astride her, his masculine center pressed into her derriere, and she knew he was ready for her.

In a moment, she would order him to move away. But not yet, not while his fingertips were exploring her bosom and his kisses tantalized the nape of her neck.

She could lie this way forever, and she could bear it not a moment longer. In an instant she would yield or she would throw him off. Kim could no longer decide which, and the balance was tipping in favor of yielding.

As Jack straddled her hips, his hands caught her shoulders and turned her beneath him. The contact became shockingly intimate, his body tight to hers at its most vulnerable point while her breasts lay bare before him and her mouth opened to receive his probing kiss.

With a groan of surrender, Kim caught his powerful forearms and clung to him, arching until his ski sweater brushed across her chest. She wanted to strip away the clothes and burrow into him.

He released her for a moment, to tear away his sweater. Firelight gleamed on his broad chest and tapered waist as she helped him release the catch to his jeans.

"Are you sure you want to do this?" he whispered, his eyes hooded.

"Don't ask me that." She wanted passion to claim them both, without any thought of consequences. "Hold me, Jack."

He bent over her, within inches of claiming her. Yet he was not moving against her with the eagerness of a lover, but withdrawing into himself, caught in a battle between his desires and his honor.

The stillness forced Kim to face what she wanted to forget. If she followed her impulses, where would it lead? Jack could not stay with her. If a child resulted, which of them would it belong to? And how long would it take for the sweet passion raging between them to sour into resentment?

She did not merely want this man for one night or a few nights. If they were united, it must be forever.

For one aching moment, she found herself hoping that he would claim her without remorse. Tonight, she knew she wanted to be taken.

But he was Prince Jacques, a man who always considered the consequences of his actions and the welfare of his kingdom. And above all, whether he was keeping faith with his personal code of conduct.

So she wasn't surprised when he pulled away and began fastening his clothes. Not surprised, but keenly disappointed.

JACK LAY AWAKE into the early morning hours, too wired to relax on the lumpy double bed in the smaller bedroom. Outside, an owl punctuated his fevered musings with mournful cries.

He had never imagined he could want a woman this much. Today he had felt unfamiliar emotions, not only sexual urges but that boyish eagerness to flaunt his skill on the slopes. He had wanted to impress Kim and outmaneuver her and overwhelm her.

But it would be impossible for her to bear his child, give it up and then go on with her life. Impossible, he supposed, for both of them.

This marriage must be rethought and renegotiated. Perhaps a way could be found for Kim to take up the position of Princess of Lindelor on a permanent basis.

First, of course, they must deal with the threat from Zakovia. And she must be given full information, so she could choose freely.

The prospect of bringing her home, of drawing her into his palace and his life, helped calm his restless tossing. He didn't know how the issue of her career would be resolved, but surely a way could be found.

He had fallen in love with her, and he thought that

she loved him too. Surely her response tonight had demonstrated that.

Jack closed his eyes, feeling again the smoothness of her skin and hearing the sharp intake of her breath as he bent over her. His body came erect again, ready for her, in defiance of his resolve.

He must sleep. Tomorrow, he would need all his wits when he brought his proposal to Kim.

What seemed like a moment later, he awoke to the sweep of sunshine across the quilt. Surprised, Jack rolled over and checked the clock. It was after nine.

Embarrassed at his slothfulness, he hurried into the bathroom and cleaned up. Only when his hair was freshly combed and he'd chosen an outfit for the day did he saunter out to have a frank discussion with his wife.

She was not, he discovered when he reached the kitchen, alone.

Across from her at the small table, drinking a cup of coffee and consuming a pastry, sat the swarthy Ladislaw Munchen. The aide, his bulldog frame not quite properly fitting into its business suit, hulked over the princess. Jack felt an instinctive lurch of alarm at the sight.

Leaning back with feet propped on an empty chair, Kim looked the quintessential American. On her sweatshirt was imprinted the name of a local ice-hockey team, while her open expression showed that she felt not the least intimidated.

Morning sunlight rioted through her red-gold curls. A sprinkling of freckles had popped out across her nose in response to yesterday's glare of sun on snow.

"Good morning." She swung her feet lazily to the floor. "Did you sleep well?"

"Tolerably." Jack gave the assistant a short nod as the man jumped to his feet. "What brings you here, Herr Munchen?"

"Please forgive the intrusion, Your Highness." The dark-haired man produced a sheaf of papers. "Some new contracts arrived that require your signature."

"They could have waited a few days." Taking the papers, Jack poured himself a cup of coffee. "Why isn't Hans handling this?"

The assistant appeared to be framing his response carefully. "The foreign minister has been incommunicado since yesterday."

This information alarmed Jack until he realized what was meant. "With a certain lady, may I assume?"

Ladislaw nodded. Kim pressed her lips together to stifle a grin.

"Nevertheless, this doesn't constitute an emergency," Jack said as he riffled through the documents. "Didn't it occur to you that coming here was indiscreet? You might have been followed."

"By whom?" Kim asked.

"Anyone. The press, perhaps." Jack berated himself silently for revealing too much, but he wished Ladislaw hadn't come. Still, he saw as he finished reading one of the contracts, it would be advantageous to execute these as quickly as possible. One of Lindelor's factories was operating at half capacity, and would benefit from a quick influx of new orders.

He signed and handed the papers to the assistant. Ladislaw executed two deep bows, one to each of them, and departed.

"What an intense man," Kim observed when he

was gone. "He certainly seems dedicated to his work."

"What did you two find to talk about?" Jack asked as he ate breakfast.

"He was telling me how his grandfather fled Zakovia at the start of World War II," Kim said. "The family was very grateful to Lindelor for taking them in."

"I didn't know he was part Zakovian." The information troubled Jack, although he tried not to show it. And it didn't necessarily mean anything. Two generations of Ladislaw's family had grown up in Lindelor, after all. "How do you feel today? Stiff and sore?"

"Not as much as I expected," Kim said. "In fact, I'm eager to get out there and learn more."

Eager as he was to discuss changing their temporary marriage into a permanent one, it was a delicate subject and Jack didn't want to rush the conversation. Better to leave it for a more leisurely moment. "Let's go, then."

The slopes were almost empty, and over the next few hours Kim made considerable progress on her snowplow stops and traverse exercises. At lunchtime, they retreated to the lodge and piled their plates high in the cafeteria line.

"This is a good time to knock off. The place is starting to fill up," Jack pointed out.

Kim stretched her legs and winced. "I hope I haven't overdone it, but that was fun. This afternoon, if you want to hit the harder slopes, I'll lounge around and watch."

A warning bell went off in Jack's mind. He had left her alone for a few minutes at their wedding reception, and she'd nearly been killed. Although the ski lodge had seemed safe enough yesterday, Ladislaw's appearance that morning had made him wary.

"Let's go for a walk instead," he suggested. "We can explore the town and it will give us a chance to talk."

"About what?" Kim asked.

"Some ideas I had."

"Hmm," was the reply as she finished drinking her hot chocolate.

A short time later, they set out together through a mountain village that reminded Jack somewhat of Lindelor. Inspired by Swiss chalets, the shops and houses seemed vaguely familiar and yet foreign at the same time. It was like going back to a place many years later and discovering that it no longer matched one's memories.

The shops carried clothing, ski gear and tourist trinkets, none of which interested Kim, so after a while the two of them took a trail through the woods. Jack realized that he'd been so absorbed in rehearsing what he had to say that he hadn't paid much attention to who might be nearby. He was glad for the solitude offered by the countryside.

A blue jay flashed across the snow. "I did some thinking last night," he said.

"Isn't that beautiful?" Kim pointed at the bird.

Jack nodded distractedly. "Yes, but listen. Things have changed between us."

Her expression sobered. "In what way?"

"You haven't noticed?"

"Well..." She scuffed a small snowdrift. "I don't remember how things were between us before my accident."

"Much more distant," he said.

"Then they've definitely changed." Kim tilted her head back, letting the sun's warmth bathe her cheeks.

In an insight so piercing it almost hurt, Jack realized that he would always picture her this way, golden and vivid against the snowy landscape. A thousand shades of fire blazed in her hair and emeralds glowed with unearthly intensity in her eyes. Near her, he felt more alive than he had ever been.

"We need to rethink our marriage contract," he said.

She studied him, puzzled. "What do you mean?"

"I think you would like Lindelor." It wasn't a very romantic way to ask her to spend the rest of her life with him, Jack realized, but he was having a hard time finding the right words. "When I first met you, I made a lot of assumptions. And then, well, they seemed to be borne out."

"What kind of assumptions?"

"That you would be unsuited to my way of life," he admitted. "That as a career-oriented American woman you would never consider actually becoming my wife, in the deepest sense. But I think perhaps I was wrong."

"Wrong?" her voice quavered slightly. "About the career part or—"

"The wife part," he said.

She braced herself on the path. "Are you proposing to me?"

"I know it's a lot to ask." Jack felt like a boy asking out a girl on whom he had a terrible crush, too afraid of rejection to pause for breath. He wanted to stop the words from tumbling over each other, but his heart had a will of its own. "You would have to give up a great deal and put your trust in me. But I promise you, Kim…"

He stopped, finally becoming aware of a sound that had been buzzing at the edges of his awareness for several seconds. It was a motorized roar, coming toward them along the path.

"Doggone snowmobiles," Kim muttered. "You'd think people would stay in the city if they want all that noise."

Jack's gut twisted as he made an urgent survey of their surroundings. They stood on a narrow trail bounded by a thick screen of trees and bushes. Just ahead, a clearing opened. "Come on!"

He caught Kim's hand and pulled her. She ran with him, laughing, unaware of any potential danger.

Jack hoped he was merely being paranoid. After all, he didn't see how the Zakovians could hope to kill Kim and disguise it as an accident with him as a witness.

He supposed they might intend for the accident to take his life as well, but they must know the Lindelorians would refuse to honor the treaty if there was any question that he had been assassinated. And after Kim's earlier accident and the near collision Hans had experienced, there would certainly be questions.

But none of that mattered. The only thing he cared about was getting Kim to safety.

When she stumbled, Jack caught her under the arms and yanked her the final half-dozen feet until they could plunge off the path. He caught the shock in her eyes as she realized he was not joking.

"Jack?" she said. "What's going on?"

"Nothing, I hope." He pulled her into the small

opening, and then realized he'd made a terrible mistake.

Where the path had been lined by a thick but not impenetrable tangle, the clearing was surrounded by hard-packed drifts as high as his shoulders. Whoever had cleared the path had pushed the excess snow into this space and shoved it into a solid encircling wall.

They were trapped.

"Quick." He formed a stirrup with his hands. "I have to boost you over..."

The whine of snowmobiles rose into a roar as two vehicles slammed into the clearing. Bundled in heavy clothing, the riders wore ski masks that made them impossible to identify.

The snowmobiles spun to a halt, sending up a swathe of whiteness. Desperately, Jack seized Kim and tried to throw her over the wall of snow. Scrabbling in vain for a handhold, she slid back down.

For a frozen instant, the assassins confronted them across the small clearing. One was slender, not much more than a boy. The other had a chunky build. They both pulled guns.

"Keep them covered," rasped the heavier man. "I'll set our little scene."

"No." Jack moved in front of Kim.

"Who—who are these people?" she quavered.

"I don't know."

"Zakovians," she whispered. "Aren't they?"

There was no point in trying to keep secrets any longer. "Yes." To the intruders, he said, "If you shoot us, the treaty is forfeit."

"I have no intention of shooting you, Your Highness." The man's voice dripped sarcasm as he pulled a syringe from his pocket. "Just let go of the woman and you'll come out of this not much the worse for wear.''

Feverishly, Jack's mind flicked over the possibilities. The syringe must contain drugs. In a horrified flash, he visualized the scenario authorities would find: two people high on drugs, the woman accidentally killed by a hit-and-run snowmobiler, the man too incoherent to be a credible witness.

"You'll have to kill me," he said.

"Don't be a damn fool." As the man raised his gun threateningly, his cap pulled back to reveal a hank of red hair.

"That man!" Kim said. "He was changing a tire near the doctor's office."

"Hurry up!" snarled the youth on the snowmobile. "Just shoot them."

"Don't be an idiot!" The red-haired man waved his gun at Jack. "Let her go and spare yourself!"

Faced with just one foe, it might have been a standoff. But Jack's instincts told him the youth was too impulsive to weigh the consequences of an outright assassination. In another minute, the kid would start firing.

He had to bring the heavy man down and get his gun, and he had to do it now. "Duck!" he yelled at Kim, and dived toward the man's legs.

In that instant, a shot rang out overhead, loud as a cannon. Then Jack slammed into the red-haired man and they went down onto the snow-packed ground. He heard a scream from behind him. Kim's scream, and then only silence.

He hadn't been fast enough. He hadn't been honest enough. He should have told her the truth and let her go. If he had, she would still be alive.

The stocky man was strong, but Jack quickly discovered that his opponent had no experience in hand-to-hand combat. Within seconds, Jack wrapped the villain's arm behind his back and twisted the gun loose.

At every instant, he expected the other assassin to send a bullet plowing through his body. Instead, he heard the roar of a motor and looked up in time to see the youth flying away down the path.

With a string of curses, the stocky man abandoned his gun and lurched free. Remembering the syringe, Jack hesitated, and in that frozen moment his attacker leaped onto the snowmobile. By the time Jack recovered enough to snatch up the gun, the man was zooming away.

His finger wavered on the trigger. Shooting a fleeing attacker still constituted murder. More important, Jack had to see to Kim.

Fear squeezing his heart, he turned toward his wife. She crouched near the bank, her eyes wide with fear. But she was alive.

"Are you hurt?" Pocketing the gun, he hurried over and knelt beside her.

She shook her head. "I don't think so."

"I heard a shot. I don't see how he could have missed you."

"That was my shot," said a man's voice. Above them, snow tumbled off the top of the drift, as if someone were coming over it.

Jack started back in alarm. "Who is it?"

"It's me, Your Highness." Ladislaw dropped to the ground, holding a revolver.

"What are you doing here?"

"When I left your house this morning, I noticed a

car sitting across the street." The aide resembled a bulldog more than ever. A loyal, dependable bulldog. "I wasn't sure there was anything wrong, but I thought I'd better stick around."

"You've been following us all day?" Jack asked.

"I hope I wasn't presumptuous."

"Presumptuous?" Kim found her voice. "You saved our lives!"

Jack felt a rush of shame at the suspicions he'd harbored about the aide. "I will be eternally grateful."

"I'm only glad I had the chance, Your Highness." Discreetly, Ladislaw offered Kim his arm. He must have realized Jack was unsteady on his feet after such a close brush with death.

As they walked back to town, Jack's heartbeat slowed and his thoughts began to clear. He could see now that the danger was greater than he had anticipated. Even his presence hadn't been enough to protect Kim.

And the timing of the attack couldn't have been worse. He'd been on the point of asking Kim to come back to Lindelor and live with him forever. As he recalled, he'd been saying that she needed to trust him.

Kim was still in shock. She hadn't begun to assess the implications of what had just happened.

But when she did, and when she realized how much he had withheld from her, Jack feared her likely inclination would be to never trust him again.

Chapter Ten

The trip down the mountain and back to Laguna Beach passed in a blur. Seated next to Jack, with Ladislaw following in another car, Kim couldn't stop flinching at every noise and expected to see machine guns poke out of oncoming vehicles.

She felt the same unreasoning terror that gripped her whenever she tried to recall the scene at the hotel just after her wedding. All she knew was that both times someone had tried to kill her.

And she realized now Jack must have been aware of the danger. That was why he'd insisted on having someone accompany her everywhere.

No wonder Hans had been so shaken by their near collision outside Newport Center. And she could also understand why Jack had refused to pass the truck on a narrow curve as they left the doctor's office.

All this time she'd been in deadly peril, and he had hidden it from her. Had he only been trying to protect her, or was he hoping to trick her into having his baby by keeping her unaware of the truth?

She turned to observe Jack as he piloted the car with grim concentration. In profile, his jaw was set and his eyes burned with intensity.

He had been more or less proposing to her when the accident occurred. But she didn't see how she could ever rely on him again. He'd had no right to keep her in a state of ignorance, not when her life was at stake.

A shudder ran through Kim. Would she ever be out of danger? As long as she lived, she might pose a threat to Prince Igor. Or would she be safe once she got a divorce?

Just then they rounded a bend and began a long, curving descent alongside a sheer drop of hundreds of feet. She could barely see the valley floor below.

Would someone attempt to ram them? Thank goodness Ladislaw was following, but judging by the way those assassins had come prepared with syringes as well as guns, they might appear at any moment in heavy trucks or have planted a land mine or...

"Kim," Jack said. "Your eyes are glazing over."

She released a long breath. "I can't stop thinking about what happened."

"Neither can I," he admitted. "It pains me to admit it, but I underestimated Prince Igor."

"You're sure he was behind this?"

"Unfortunately, yes."

She'd known, of course, that the Zakovians would eventually get Lindelor after Jack died, if he didn't have a child by a noblewoman. "But he wouldn't benefit for decades. Maybe longer."

"Don't be so sure," Jack said. "Once the possibility of my producing an heir is eliminated, he isn't above extortion. Igor could ride herd on our contracts, demand payments from us for agreeing to co-sign them, even borrow against our assets. He could undermine the Lindelorian economy so that by the time Kristoffer inherits it, there would be nothing left.''

''Can't you annul the treaty?'' Kim asked. ''I mean, 1815 was a long time ago.''

Jack shook his head. ''If we did that without justification, he'd have an excuse to go to war. In today's fragmented world, I'm sure he'd find allies eager to acquire Lindelor's medical industry. Even if we won, the cost would be enormous.''

She leaned back, wondering how she'd ever landed in such a quagmire. Even trying to be charitable, she couldn't avoid the conclusion that this was Jack's fault. He should have warned her before they were married.

It hurt to realize that their growing closeness mattered so little that, this morning, he had still led her blindly into peril. Well, perhaps that wasn't quite fair. The simple truth was that the good of his country mattered more to him than Kim's well-being and always would. She supposed she might feel the same way if Lindelor were her country. But it wasn't.

''I think we should notify the police,'' she said at last. Immediately after the attack, she'd been too stunned to argue with Jack's insistence that they leave at once, but her good sense was reasserting itself. ''They might be able to track these people down.''

He grimaced. ''How? We didn't get any identifying information off the snowmobiles. We couldn't even see their faces, let alone prove they're from Zakovia. And since no one got hurt, it wouldn't be a high priority for your authorities.''

''At least we could let them know what's going on,'' Kim pointed out.

''All that would do is create an international incident and bring down the media," Jack warned. "They would camp out on your doorstep and pester you for weeks, months, maybe years. And then there's the matter of Ladislaw illegally carrying a weapon."

At the mention of the aide, Kim fell silent. She certainly didn't want to cause trouble for the man who had saved her life and Jack's.

After another half hour of heart-stopping curves above sheer cliffs, the road straightened. Kim wished her own inner path were as clear.

Part of her yearned to resume the life she had known and could remember now with only a few blank spots: working in real estate, seeing her family on weekends, playing on the beach, enjoying quiet pursuits. Yet the previous night Jack had awakened a part of her that was unlikely to go quietly back to sleep.

She couldn't trust him. But she wasn't sure she could let go of him, either.

"I've called ahead and arranged for your aunt to meet us at your apartment," said the prince. "You need some emotional support, receiving a shock like this while you're still recuperating. We're also posting two security guards from our trade mission."

"How about you?" she asked. "What are you planning to do?"

"My staff and I need to go over the facts and make some assessments."

Kim's inner warning system went on alert. "Not without me, you don't. No more keeping me in the dark."

After a moment's reflection, Jack said, "You're right. But there are some sensitive security matters involved, and until you commit yourself to Lindelor we can't tell you everything."

Kim could see his point. "I just need to know the stuff that concerns me."

He slanted her a warm look. "You really do have the makings of a princess, you know. You're handling this with a lot of grace. Most people would be calling me names by now."

"I'm just too numb to think of any."

A low chuckle was the response. "Well, I promise to give you all relevent information and present you with whatever options we come up with. And you can call me all relevant names when you think of them."

"Give me a preview," she said. "What steps do you think you'll recommend?"

Jack hesitated. "I haven't given it much thought."

She could feel anger flaming her cheeks. Was the man intentionally trying to frustrate her? "You're doing it again! Treating me like an idiot! You must have some idea what you plan to do, and I have a right to know what it is."

In Jack's startled gaze, she saw emotions warring. Then he said, "All right. I've been thinking you should come back to Lindelor with me for the swimming-and-diving competition."

"For how long?" she asked.

"Until it seems safe for you to return."

The idea of visiting Lindelor held a certain appeal, Kim mused. She would enjoy meeting Angela again, and seeing the picturesque village that her grandfather had described. And what little girl doesn't dream, at least once, of living in a palace?

It was a life that Kim Norris, title rep, had never

coveted or imagined. But during the past week the idea had piqued her curiosity.

Then she remembered how close she'd come the night before to making love with Jack. Once, she had considered herself self-sufficient enough to bear his child and then go on by herself.

But the previous night's close encounter had revealed her vulnerability. Once she was in his country and his castle, might she not be lulled into forgetting her own interests and agreeing to remain as princess? What if she woke up too late, after they had children, and realized she was pretending to be someone she wasn't?

"I can't go," she said. "I'm sorry I haven't found the money yet, but we have to proceed with the divorce."

"We will." Jack's expression was subdued and hard to read. "This is just a way to protect you for the next few weeks."

"Surely there's some other way."

"I'll discuss it with my staff," he said. "But promise me you'll at least think about it."

It was obvious they couldn't resolve the point right this minute. "I *will* think about it, if you insist. But don't get your hopes up."

The chill weather of the mountains yielded to the warmth of the lowlands as they drove. Between the comfortable temperature, the vibration of the car and her own exhaustion, Kim fell asleep.

She awoke with a start, disoriented and alarmed, as the car halted and two men threw open the doors. Before she could scream, however, Kim realized Jack was calling the men by name. With their help, she stepped out and let her husband take her arm.

Blinking, she saw that they were in the alley behind her apartment. The two men were escorting her and the prince up the steps while keeping a sharp watch for interference.

The door opened and Valerie welcomed them inside, concern creasing her forehead. "Thank goodness you're all right! We were so frightened."

Behind her, Hans nodded gravely. "I feel partly to blame. I haven't been paying much attention to business lately."

Valerie winced at the comment. "And I've been distracting him. But I had no idea you might be in danger, Kim." The tall woman gave her niece a hug.

"Neither did I," Kim admitted.

"There's plenty of blame to go around, but most of it belongs to me," Jack said as he guided her to the couch.

Valerie fixed him with her gray gaze, which over the years had intimidated renegade journalists, quibbling advertisers and a flaky male model who finally decided to honor his contract after all. "It certainly does. You had no business dragging my niece into your crazy Balkan politics."

Hans grimaced. "Lindelor is not in the Balkans. It's in the Alps."

"It was a figure of speech!" retorted the editor. "Don't you think I know a little basic geography? And if the two of you dream up any more darn fool plans involving my niece, I expect you to let us know *before* the bullets start flying."

"There were no bullets." Hans drew himself up stiffly, defending his prince. "Or rather, the bullets were only incidental."

"Incidental?" roared Valerie. "I'd like to see you

dismiss bullets as 'incidental' if they were aimed at you! That's the most pompous, arrogant—"

"Pompous?" snapped the foreign minister. "Arrogant? Is that what you think of me, madame?"

Jack interjected himself between the two. "Miss Norris, I assure you, I'm doing everything possible to protect your niece."

The strain of the past few hours showed in Valerie's brittle tone. "Why should I trust you? You're the one who dragged her into this mess in the first place."

"She agreed to be 'dragged into this mess' for a million dollars, I might point out," retorted the foreign minister.

"The money isn't the issue," Jack said tightly.

"It certainly isn't!" agreed Valerie. "All right, go play your games. But I'll make sure Kim's rights are protected, if I have to hire a lawyer to do it!"

"I can see you have the typical American tendency to overlitigate!" Before Hans could continue, Jack caught his arm and tugged him from the apartment.

"Insufferable man!" Valerie glared at the door for several seconds. Then, looking away, she encountered her niece's amused gaze.

"Insufferable?" said Kim.

Valerie chuckled. "That is rather quaint language, isn't it? I wonder what on earth made me talk that way."

"You must be in love."

Her aunt drew back in mock horror. "Heaven forbid! Oh, dear, there's another archaic term. The man is turning me into a Victorian anachronism. And now, Jack was right about one thing. You should lie down."

"I slept in the car," Kim said, but didn't object

when her aunt steered her into the bedroom. Her eyelids kept drooping, so she decided to lie down for a minute or two.

The next thing she knew, twilight had fallen. Sitting up, she felt muscles tug and creak from unaccustomed use on the ski slope. The sensation was more pleasant than painful.

Wondering if any decisions had been made during her absence, she cleaned up and went into the living room. There she found Valerie and Siegfried playing Scrabble on the coffee table.

"Your Highness!" The valet jumped up. "I should have been attending to supper."

"He's been sitting here for ten minutes, trying to figure out how to get a triple word score," grumbled Valerie. "Next time we play, I'm insisting on a timer."

While Siegfried hurried into the kitchen, Kim's aunt gestured her onto the sofa. "How do you feel?"

"A little stiff," she said. "Look, I hope I didn't cause trouble between you and Hans."

"I suppose we've broken up." Valerie's brown hair lay loose around her shoulders and she wore more makeup than usual. The effect was to make her look softer and more feminine. "I suppose it was inevitable."

"Why?"

"Because his work is in Lindelor, and mine is here," her aunt said. "Besides, we're two crusty middle-aged people used to getting our own ways and setting our own agendas. I really like him, but I knew it couldn't last." The tension in her voice told Kim what her aunt couldn't say, that she had hoped against hope that they could work things out.

It seemed safer to change the subject. "Are my parents upset about the attack?"

"I didn't tell them," her aunt admitted. "I thought I'd leave that decision to you. Your father has so many business worries, as it is. Well, with any luck, you'll soon be single again and out of harm's way."

Single again. The words reverberated in Kim's mind. She kept seeing images of Jack leaning over her hospital bed, emerging from the surf, flashing down the ski slope while the onlookers gasped.

Mostly, she recalled the warmth in his smile when they were alone together, and the sudden shyness when he broached the idea of making their marriage permanent. How could she ever hope to meet a man as special again?

It was a relief when Siegfried entered with a tray from which issued the enticing scents of dinner. Kim decided that for one more evening at least she would enjoy the perks of being a princess. And this meal was definitely one of them.

"How could the Zakovians have known where we were?" Jack asked when he was alone in the hotel suite with Hans, Pierre and Ladislaw. "Any chance this place is bugged?"

"We sweep it electronically a couple of times a day," Pierre said. "But of course they could be snooping from a distance."

"There's always the possibility you were followed to the mountains," noted Ladislaw. "Or that I was, although I took precautions."

"So did I." Jack drummed his fingers on a desk. "Did any of us tell *anybody* where I was going?"

Hans shook his head. "I didn't even discuss it with Valerie."

"What about Kim's boss, the one who owns the cabin?" said Pierre.

"I called him a few minutes ago," said Ladislaw. "He hasn't mentioned it to anyone."

"As far as I can see, the only people who knew were the four of us, Kim's boss and Siegfried." Jack didn't like the implication that someone in his inner circle must be involved. "Who else? Think hard, people."

"Angela," said Ladislaw.

"Excuse me?" asked the foreign minister, his thin features even sharper than usual.

"She called with some questions about the schedule for the swim meet," explained the dark-haired aide. "I said you'd gone skiing in the mountains. Nothing specific."

"She might have mentioned it to Grand Duke Kristoffer," Hans said. "They've been awfully chummy."

"Angela would never be so indiscreet!" Pierre retorted. "She's as loyal as we are."

"Love sometimes leads people astray," said Ladislaw.

"She's not in love!" Jack had never seen the easygoing secretary so upset. "And she would never betray her country for that man!"

This argument was going nowhere. It was Jack's responsibility to find a solution, and he was reluctantly beginning to see where the answer lay.

Until now, he had never had difficulty handling his duties as head of Lindelor's government. But he'd never been called upon to deal with this kind of threat before, either. It was time to stop acting like the chief executive of a business and to start acting like a prince.

"Whoever these assassins are, they're clever and they're subtle," he said. "Prince Igor hasn't simply put out a contract on Kim. He's using people he knows, who understand the implications of the treaty."

The other men ceased squabbling. "Yes, Your Highness?" said Hans.

"I think if we can catch this pair, we'll at least get a breather," Jack said. "Long enough to allow time for a divorce or—whatever the princess chooses. We may even be able to link them definitively to Zakovia."

"But you can hardly bring Igor to justice," Hans pointed out.

"I can dissolve the treaty, and I will," Jack said.

"Technically, Your Highness, it wouldn't wash."

"Damn technicalities!"

The three men regarded him in astonishment, and then Ladislaw said, "We'd be free of them forever! Go for it, Your Highness!"

Pierre grinned his approval. After a moment's thought, even Hans gave a nod of agreement.

The hardest part was yet to come. "The first thing we have to do is capture them and prove what's going on," Jack said.

"How, exactly?" asked Pierre.

"That," said Jack, "is something I'll have to work out. By myself." It was going to be hard to do this alone, when his instincts shouted at him to use his management team. But either there was a leak, or someone had found a way to eavesdrop. "I'll need your help, all of you. But I'm the only one who will know all the details.''

KIM REGARDED JACK dubiously over the remains of dinner. Upon his arrival a few minutes earlier, Siegfried and Valerie had departed to allow the prince and princess a private discussion.

"You're going to set a trap?" she asked. "And let me guess what you'll be using for bait. Or should I say, *whom?*"

At least she hadn't thrown anything at him yet, Jack reflected. He wouldn't blame her.

The last thing he would ever want was to subject her to further danger. But they couldn't go on waiting for assassins to pop out of closets.

In an odd twist of fate, he realized, Kim was the only person he could trust absolutely in this matter. Her intelligence and insights might prove vital. He needed her with him one hundred percent.

"They must be associates of Igor's, people he knows well," he said. "If you accompany me back to the swim meet, he'll send them to Lindelor. It would seem natural, since they'll have a team competing."

"So what will you do, arrest any red-haired men who show up?" Kim challenged. "I suspect they have hair dyes in Zakovia."

Stretching legs stiff from skiing, Jack leaned forward in his chair and tried to ignore the scent of food stirring his hunger pangs. He wasn't in the mood to eat, not yet. "We won't be able to do anything until they attack. But at least we'll be on home ground, and we'll be offering only a narrow window of opportunity. That improves our chances of success considerably.''

Guilt gripped his heart as he watched the sadness and indecision on her face. Until his arrival a few weeks earlier, Kim had enjoyed a carefree existence. Now she was facing a life-or-death decision, with no easy way out.

"You really think you could dissolve the treaty?" she said.

"If I can prove Prince Igor was behind an assassination attempt on Lindelorian soil, I'll do it," Jack assured her. "I doubt he'd be able to stir up support for a war once he's exposed as a terrorist."

"And then—we'd both be free." She pronounced the words with uncharacteristic flatness.

"I promise you this," he said. "Come back with me for a week, and then whether or not we catch anyone you can have a divorce. And keep the million dollars. If you're still in danger, I'll throw in two armed guards for as long as you want."

She sat motionless, her chin resting on her palm, her expression distant. Jack would have given a great deal to read her thoughts. But he was glad she couldn't read his.

Somewhere along the line, he had fallen in love with his princess. Until now, his need to produce an heir and his hunger to possess her had dovetailed, so he hadn't had to examine the implications of his feelings.

But he had just given his word. If the treaty with Zakovia were dissolved, he could no longer try to maneuver her into remaining in the marriage. He would have to give up the only woman he had ever loved.

There was always the possibility he could make her change her mind and stay with him. But that didn't seem likely.

He almost hoped she would turn down the idea of setting a trap. Then he wouldn't be obligated to release her until they had a child, and that would give him more precious time to win both her affections and trust.

From her frown, he thought she was going to say no. No to Lindelor, but also no to an instant divorce. His spirits began to rise, until the princess lifted her chin in an unconsciously regal manner and her green eyes bored into his.

"Let's go for it," she said.

Chapter Eleven

On the long flight to Lindelor, Kim was keenly aware of Hans and Pierre occupying nearby seats, keeping a close eye on her and Jack. Siegfried sat in the back, baby-sitting their hand luggage, while Ladislaw had remained in Los Angeles to finish up a trade pact.

Sometimes she thought she must be crazy to have agreed to this arrangement. Other times, it seemed like the only possible decision.

They had to confront the danger in order to end it. Then at last she would really be free, not only of obligation but of a sense of guilt. If the treaty were dissolved, Lindelor wouldn't suffer for her decision not to serve as a surrogate mother.

And neither would Jack. Despite his tenderness in the mountains, Kim had reluctantly concluded that he was too political a person ever to separate his feelings for her from the welfare of his country.

It hurt to realize that, however much he might be drawn to her, the main attraction was her ability to give him an heir who would earn the Zakovian seal of approval. Angela would have done as well, and so would any other distant relative his aides might some-day dredge up.

At least his promise to let her keep the money would help someone she loved. At the airport before she left, her father's face had been gray and drawn. From Valerie, Kim knew that he was barely staving off bankruptcy.

The most frustrating part was that with his rights to the patent finally secured her father stood on the brink of being able to make the fortune he'd always dreamed of. But without investment capital all would be lost.

Kim hoped he would never find out the role she was playing on his behalf. He would be horrified if he knew his daughter had put herself at risk in order to help his business.

Now she just had to remember where she'd put the money. She hoped that, after a week in Lindelor, the last pieces of her memory would drop into place when she returned to Laguna.

In Zurich, they changed to a small commuter aircraft. Beside her, Jack stretched in a vain effort to uncramp his large frame.

"I'm glad you're coming at this time of year. Spring is our most beautiful season." He brushed an errant strand of red-gold hair from her temple.

Kim fought the urge to lean against him. Not only were the two Lindelorian officials close by, but the plane also carried a couple of Chinese athletes and their coaches arriving for the competition, only three days away. She had to remember that she and Jack were, in a sense, public figures.

After angling through a mountain pass so narrow Kim didn't see how the wings could avoid brushing the slopes on either side, the plane cleared the mountains. They swept over fields and streams brilliant with blues and greens and snowy masses of sheep swarming the high pastures.

Past the fields, white cottages gleamed in the sunlight, interspersed with red-and-yellow flower gardens. In the center of town stood a bell tower, also white, dominating a rectangular plaza on which a bright mosaic depicted the legendary wolf that appeared on the Lindelorian flag.

To one side, sunlight sparkled off an Olympic-size pool beside a huge domed structure. Kim guessed the building must house the indoor pool and athletic facilities. Adjacent to it arose a three-story structure that she recognized from a travel brochure as the Hotel de Lindelor.

Beyond, on a rise of ground that must command a magnificent view, green banners snapped from the battlements of an ivory castle. Its walls sheltered an alabaster palace and a meandering pool rimmed by trees.

From its front gate, Kim could make out tiny horses pulling a red cart toward the village. "Your people still use horses?"

Gazing over her shoulder, Jack said, "We prefer them, although we do have cars and trams. And in good weather people walk. You can do that when your country covers only about eighteen square miles."

His face radiated warmth for his country. And who could blame him? Kim thought. It was like a fairy tale come true.

As the plane landed at a small airport, she had the odd sense that she was coming home. She'd heard so many stories about Lindelor from her grandfather that she couldn't wait to see its landmarks.

A small knot of officials awaited them on the tarmac. As she and Jack descended the steps, Kim saw that a red carpet had been spread for them to walk on. Then a little girl thrust a bouquet of flowers into her arms, bobbed a nervous curtsy and dashed away.

"How sweet!" Kim sniffed the bouquet appreciatively, then realized she was keeping everyone waiting. Starting forward, she said, "I'm not used to this kind of treatment."

Jack assumed a pleasantly dignified expression for the sole photographer, an aged man wearing an embroidered blouse, olive-green suspenders and formfitting knee breeches. The man clicked the photo and then made a respectful bow to the accompaniment of popping and cracking joints.

The prince nodded politely, and Kim beamed at the funny-looking fellow. He gave her an answering smile full of genuine friendliness.

"There's a small reception in your honor tonight at the palace," said Jack as he guided her away. "I hope it will be a relaxed occasion. Our foreign guests haven't arrived yet."

"A reception?" With a sinking sensation, Kim realized she hadn't given much thought to her wardrobe. She'd worn one of her best suits and packed the other, along with the gown from the Zakovian ball. She suspected those would be woefully inadequate for the days ahead.

"Did I mention that Siegfried has been doing some shopping on your behalf?" murmured her husband as they strolled toward an open carriage. "I hope you'll approve."

"I'm sure I will." Kim gazed in delight at the two

ebony horses that waited in harness. "These are beautiful!"

"We take pride in our stables. Actually, I helped train them myself."

As a footman held the door, Jack handed her into the carriage. He swung into place beside Kim and off they rattled over the cobblestone streets of Lindelor, leaving Hans, Pierre and Siegfried to follow in a car.

People lined the sidewalks, cheering and snapping pictures. Trying not to look as self-conscious as she felt, Kim waved and smiled back.

She noticed several young women regarding her as if scrutinizing every detail of her hair and clothing. "They'll be whipping up suits like yours and getting their hair cut tomorrow," advised Jack.

"Oh, no!" Kim's hand flew to her rumpled curls. "I was thinking of letting it grow!"

"Like it or not, you're a role model now," he said.

They passed several clinics and a pharmaceutical company, all built with the traditional peaked roofs and whitewashed walls. At every window, boxes overflowed with colorful blossoms.

What fascinated Kim were the spots she recognized from her grandfather's reminiscences. She picked out a triangular cottage with green shutters that bore a sign advertising sweets and bonbons. That must be the candy store where Grandpa had worked sixty years ago before emigrating.

When she told Jack, he said, "Why did he leave?"

"He was worried about the Nazis," Kim explained. "He thought they might overrun Lindelor."

Her husband nodded. "We were lucky they left us alone. But why didn't he return?"

"He married my grandmother." Kim could still see

their faces and hear their voices from years ago, bright and peppery as they teased each other. "To you, it must seem peculiar for a man to give up his country for a woman."

"Not all that peculiar," said Jack.

At last they headed to higher ground between rows of flowering trees. The air was full of perfume and the hum of bees.

"I suppose Lindelor makes its own honey," Kim said.

"Four varieties." Her husband smiled. "You can sample them all."

"I'd like to take some home for my parents," she said without thinking, and saw his expression shade into remoteness at the reminder that she was soon to leave.

"Of course," he said.

Over a small bridge they clattered, above a placid stream. Rolling between the palace's outer walls, they entered a kidney-shaped courtyard where the horses pulled to a halt.

Kim blinked, trying to get her bearings. The palace was laid out in an irregular manner, with a large central building flanked by smaller wings, all designed of curving shapes and iridescent colors. Some passageways had greenhouse panels thrown open to the spring air, revealing orange and lemon trees inside.

"It's like one vast garden," she said as a footman helped her out of the carriage.

"There's nowhere else like it." Jack descended with graceful agility. "Our great-great-grandmother designed it."

As if a signal had been given—and perhaps it had—people poured from the building to form a re-

ception line. A few wore traditional Swiss-style costumes. Others were garbed in uniforms of hunter
green, the women wearing frilled aprons over their
dresses.

Then there were ladies and gentlemen in exqui-
sitely tailored garments. Kim hoped they had dressed
up to greet the prince and didn't always look this
formal.

Their faces blurred together, but she made an effort
to greet each one individually as Jack did. At last he
whisked her into the palace, through vast rooms and
long corridors, to an expansive bedchamber decorated
in the colors of sunrise.

"You'll want to rest before the reception," he said.
"I'll have a supper tray brought to you."

Taking Kim's hand, he placed a kiss on the palm.
She felt a tingle run through her, but before she could
respond he was gone.

Tired but too excited to sleep, Kim wandered into
the bathroom, which was as large as her living room
at home. A velour robe and several towels had been
laid out, along with an array of oils, soaps and sham-
poos. With a deep sigh, she began to run the bath.

When she emerged, she found that her suitcases
had been unpacked. An armoire stood partly open,
revealing not only her familiar garments but an array
of fabrics she'd never seen before.

Too tired to investigate, Kim lay down and fell
instantly asleep. She awoke to twilight and a rustling
that told her someone else was in the room.

"Hello?" She sat up.

"Your Highness." Across the room, a lady in a
peach gown curtsied, then arose and switched on a
lamp. In its soft glow, Kim could see that the woman

was in her fifties, with formally arranged blond hair. "I am Lady Nanette Orreforres, your chief lady-in-waiting."

"That's a ceremonial position, isn't it?" Kim asked. The woman certainly didn't carry herself like a servant.

"Yes. It's considered an honor." As the woman approached, Kim saw that she had a motherly, cheerful face. "I wouldn't have intruded, but Jack—the prince—thought you might appreciate some assistance in preparing for the reception."

As she swung to her feet Kim discovered she felt quite refreshed, considering the long journey. "Do you know him well?"

"Jack? Well, he's a cousin," said the lady.

"Does that make you my cousin, too?"

"Distantly." Lady Nanette possessed an energetic eagerness that kept her constantly in motion. "What a splendid wardrobe you have! But if you don't mind my saying so, we must do something about your hair. Now let me summon your supper, and then we'll see what's what."

After a light meal, they selected a blue-green gown, a diamond necklace, earrings and tiara, and silver shoes. As she styled Kim's hair with expert hands, Lady Nanette chattered away about the people and manners of the court. She seemed to have something positive to say about everyone.

"There's none of the back stabbing that you'll find at Zakovia," she said. "People here feel like a family. Of course, when you get right down to it, we *are* mostly related."

"There really isn't any other woman of marriageable age?" Kim asked. "Besides Angela, I mean?"

"Actually, there are two first cousins," said Lady Nanette. "One's eighteen and the other's thirty-eight and divorced. But such a close relationship violates both custom and law. I believe it's the same in your country."

"Well, yes," Kim said.

"We don't want to get too inbred, which is always a danger in such a small country," her lady-in-waiting continued, blow-drying Kim's rebellious curls into a civilized arrangement. "Finding you was a tremendous coup. We're all so pleased you've come home."

"But—" Kim hesitated. Did these people not realize she'd only accompanied Jack on a temporary basis?

"It's quite a cause for celebration," Lady Nanette went on. "We're doing our best to learn American customs to make you feel at ease. The cook has even mastered fried chicken and hush puppies. You do like them, don't you?"

"My favorites," said Kim, although she only ate fried chicken at fast-food restaurants and wasn't quite sure what a hush puppy was.

By the time Jack came to escort her to the reception, it was clear that no one in Lindelor realized the nature of their agreement. Kim meant to ask him about it, but forgot what she'd been thinking as soon as she saw him.

The gold-trimmed scarlet jacket and black pants emphasized his powerful frame. He seemed even taller here in this magical palace, his green eyes more brilliant as he gazed at Kim.

"You look radiant." He held out a bouquet of miniature white and red roses on a wristband. "Has Nanette been helpful?"

"She's perfect." As she slipped on the bracelet, Kim smiled at the lady-in-waiting, who curtsied with a satisfied air.

"I thought she would be," observed Jack, and offered Kim his arm.

She moved toward him, keenly aware of his familiar piney scent. His arm felt strong beneath her gloved hand, and she could barely breathe as her cheek brushed his shoulder.

Her prince had come to whisk her away. Just this once, she decided, she was going to revel in being part of a fairy tale and banish her fears and doubts to a deep, dark dungeon.

JACK COULDN'T TAKE his eyes off Kim as she mingled with the crush of guests. Even the most crotchety and hermitlike of his relatives—that would be his aunt Rapunzel—had turned out for the occasion.

Kim greeted each one with affection. She seemed delighted and a bit bemused by this outpouring of interest, and he had to admit she'd been a good sport about everyone's assumption that she intended to stay.

Perhaps it was her business experience, but she had a knack for remembering people's names. Earlier, he'd been the one whispering information into her ear. Then Angela had taken over for a while, followed by Lady Nanette. Now Kim was on her own and doing splendidly.

With her around, everything seemed fresh—the wall hangings he'd long taken for granted, the orange trees brought in from the greenhouses, even the aging orchestra playing Strauss waltzes.

Jack wished he had had time to dance with her

more than just one formal turn about the floor. But after his lengthy absence, he'd been bombarded by issues large and small, particularly involving arrangements for the swim meet.

It was his belief, shared only with Hans and Pierre, that the attack was most likely to come either during the opening ceremony or during the diving finals, when Kristoffer would be competing. Those were the only two events he and Kim were officially scheduled to attend.

Already, Jack was setting his trap. No one but he would know all the particulars. That meant that if he failed to protect her the blame rested solely on his own shoulders.

Mentally, he accepted the responsibility. But a cloud remained, darkening his thoughts. That was the real reason he'd left Kim alone so much this evening, so he wouldn't dampen her enjoyment with his own unsettled mood.

Across the room, her reddish blond hair was escaping from its demure style, wisping around her temples and sending tentative curls into space. The roses were drooping on her wristband, and Jack reminded himself that she might be suffering from jet lag.

As he approached, she was deep in conversation with the president of a large Lindelorian company that manufactured prosthetic devices.

"I should think you'd want to make your own microcomputers rather than buying them overseas," she was saying. "From what you've been telling me, it sounds like they're the wave of the future in customizing artificial limbs."

"We never considered branching into the computer business," the man admitted.

"Of course you'd have to consider the start-up costs and the patents..." Kim broke off as she spotted Jack. "I guess I'm poking my nose into matters that are none of my affair."

"Not at all." The company president wore a thoughtful expression. "Your Highness has made some interesting suggestions."

With a respectful bow he withdrew, leaving Jack to slip his arm around his wife's waist. Despite his resolve to maintain propriety, he couldn't resist nuzzling her temple and planting a kiss right on one of those rebellious wisps of hair.

"Tired?" he murmured.

She lifted a bit of lint off the gold braid on his shoulder. "I'm way past tired."

"Then we'd better get you to bed."

She didn't protest. Protocol required that they take formal leave of the assembly, so Jack signaled the orchestra to stop.

As silence fell and heads turned toward them, he apologized for the early departure and urged his guests to continue partying. But as he led Kim from the room, people began gathering their belongings and preparing to leave.

Lindelorian nobles did not like to linger and gossip, Jack reflected. They were the early-to-bed sort by nature, anyway. Within minutes, the reception room would be empty and the carriages would have departed, while those relatives who lived in the palace would be tucked into their beds watching old movies on their VCRs.

With Kim at his side, he took a circuitous route back to her room. It was one of the precautions Jack had resolved upon to minimize risk, although it bothered him to have to be so suspicious in his own home.

At the chamber, he unlocked the door and prowled inside, switching on a lamp and checking for any sign of intrusion. A maid had left Kim's nightgown atop the covers and a wrapped chocolate on her pillow, but otherwise nothing had been disturbed. The French doors leading outside were locked.

"You're worried, even here?" Her face tilted upward, the lamplight bringing out the velvety softness of her skin.

"Just being careful," Jack said. "We also have guards patrolling the corridors and the grounds. And there's an intercom by your bed. Dial 1-1 to get my room."

Kim shivered. "How far away is it?"

"Right next door."

She sat on the bed, fingering the richly woven covering. "Could you stay and talk a while? We've hardly said two words to each other tonight."

He wanted to do more than stay and talk. He wanted to lower her onto the sheets and remove her jewelry, item by item. Next would come the delicate shoes and the glittery stockings, and then that gown the color of the ocean.

From that night in the mountains, his hands retained a tactile sense of the round swell of her breasts. He knew how her body would mold itself to his and how her lips would return and deepen his kiss.

But that would be taking advantage of her trust. He had deceived and manipulated her all along, and now her life lay in danger. He had no right to make love to Kim until they could come together free of obligation or pressure.

"I—" He stopped, wondering how much he should say. Perhaps he was holding too much back. She had a right to know everything that he did. "There is something I want to explain."

"Your plans?" she asked. "I'd like to know as much as possible so I can help."

She stood before him, a slim, sensuous figure in the lamp glow. Jack stroked her shoulders with open hands. "It's best if you don't. That way, you can't accidentally reveal anything."

"I'm not a complete fool."

"No, but you have an expressive face," he said. "Half the time I can read your emotions without even trying."

"Can you?" she challenged. "Then what am I feeling right now?"

The answer caught in his throat as he took in the sparkle of her eyes and the way her mouth parted slightly. "The same thing I am," he admitted gruffly and released her. "Which is why I have to leave. Be sure to lock up when I'm gone."

Without waiting for a response, he turned and strode out, pausing only to listen for the click of the lock behind him. Damning himself for cowardice, Jack stalked down the hall to his room.

As he came in, Siegfried was plumping the pillows on the canopied bed. The valet turned toward him expectantly, then gave a small sigh as if disappointed to see Jack alone.

"Get some sleep," the prince said. "No one expects you to work twenty-four hours a day."

"I enjoy it," the valet said primly. "But I am rather bushed. If you'll just let me remove your uniform—"

"I can throw it over a chair as well as the next man," said Jack, trying not to be edgy with his devoted servant. "Now good night."

"Good night, Your Highness." Siegfried bowed and removed himself quietly from the room.

In this mood, it might be hours before he could sleep, Jack reflected as he peeled off his jacket. What he needed was a long swim in the palace pool to work off the tension.

Donning trunks and slipping his feet into sandals, he went out through the French doors. After locking them behind him, he slipped on the necklace-like key chain. He had never bothered to do this before, but he would take no chance of giving admittance to a killer.

Around him, the mild spring air carried the scents of lavender and roses. Never before had he felt uneasy at every cracking twig and rustle of a bird in a tree. There was so much at stake now, more than Jack could bear thinking about.

He passed several windows, one dark, another issuing the televised chatter of voices. From far off, he caught the rumble of wooden wheels on cobblestones and the nicker of horses as his guests departed.

Turning a corner, he nearly collided with a guard in a green uniform. Reaching for his holstered gun, the man stopped as he recognized the prince. "My apologies, Your Highness."

"Carry on," said Jack. "I'll be at the pool for a while."

"I'll see that you're not disturbed," the man answered, and saluted.

Skirting the rear of the building, Jack emerged at the pool, a natural hot spring that had been expanded and deepened. A thin cloud of steam rose into the cool air, while overhanging trees blotted out the sight of nearby buildings.

Diving in, he felt the warm water close around him. Powered by restless energy, he cut back and forth across the length of the pool, the splash of water and the pull of muscles soothing his disquiet.

He had lost track of the time or the number of laps when he heard the whisper of footsteps on the bark-covered path. The soft noise sent his heart slamming against his ribs.

One thing was for sure. Those soft steps didn't belong to the guard.

Chapter Twelve

After Jack left, Kim washed and changed into a silky amber nightgown, which had been one of Siegfried's purchases. She kept feeling that something was missing, or rather someone.

Tonight, even as she relished meeting new relatives and chatting with the aristocrats, she had felt distanced from Jack. Why had he spent so much time away from her?

It was as if he'd given up his quest to have an heir, preferring to rely upon capturing the criminals and dissolving the treaty. Perhaps it came as a relief to him, that he would be able to choose his own wife.

Staring at herself in a full-length mirror rimmed with gold, Kim couldn't help noticing the brightness in her gaze and the way the fabric clung to her body. It didn't seem possible that she could want Jack so much without his feeling the same way.

There was one advantage to being a twenty-eight-year-old American businesswoman instead of the traditional naive princess bride. Kim knew enough about men and about Jack to realize that something didn't jibe.

He was anything but indifferent to her. He wanted

her with an intensity that matched her own. And she intended to find out why he was holding back.

Lifting the intercom, she pressed 1-1. It rang a dozen times, but no one answered.

If she knocked on his door he probably wouldn't answer, either. On the other hand their patios must adjoin, and through the glass doors she might be able to tell if he was home.

Taking the key from its peg on the wall, she opened her doors and went out. Her leather-soled slippers flicked over the concrete as she crossed the space between their rooms.

Through the glass doors, she could see into the lamplit interior. His uniform had been tossed across a chair, but there was no sign of Jack.

Kim was about to turn back when a green-coated guard came down the path. "Your Highness!" He saluted. "Were you seeking the prince? He's at the pool." The man pointed. "Would you like me to escort you?"

"That won't be necessary." Surely it was safe here in this walled retreat, especially with the guard poking around.

"You should lock your doors," he cautioned, and Kim complied before taking the path.

A short time later, through a tangle of trees, she saw steam rising from a pool. For a moment she considered turning back. Obviously, Jack wanted to be alone tonight or he wouldn't have come out here.

But she had too many questions demanding answers. Soon the competition would start and there would be scarcely a moment alone with her husband.

Her husband. Not for much longer, perhaps, but they were still married tonight.

Moving quietly, she skirted a flowering bush and edged toward the water. As she came closer, she could see that the pool was of natural origin and irregular shape, apparently one of the country's hot springs.

Against its soft bubbling noise came the rhythmic swish of a swimmer. As her eyes adjusted to the dimness, Kim made out a masculine figure.

She had seen Jack cut through the water this way before, in the ocean off Laguna. Even so, it impressed her to watch how cleanly and smoothly he swam.

In the dappled light, there was something primitive about him, like a man at the dawn of time. His shoulders rippled and his body moved with the sleek, questing grace of a hunter.

The elegant prince of earlier this evening had vanished. She scarcely knew this man.

Kim took a step backward, thinking to retreat unseen, but leaves rustled beneath her foot and Jack halted. He tensed as if preparing for a fight, and then he spotted her.

"Kim?"

"I needed to talk to you." She stepped clear of the shrubbery. "You've been dodging me all evening. What's going on, Jack?"

"Just preoccupied with plans for the competition. And your safety, of course." He stroked lazily toward her, ripples drifting away like smoke rings. Kim felt his gaze rake her nightgown and realized how immodest she must look in this clingy garment. But it revealed a lot less than his trunks, she reminded herself.

"You swim so well," she said. "I'm surprised you don't compete."

A moonbeam caught the flash of regret on his face. "Who has time?"

"Were you serious about swimming once?" she ventured.

Abruptly, Jack stood. Droplets gleamed on his skin as he rose from the pool like a Greek god. "As you may have noticed, I'm a competitive person. Swimming in summer, skiing in winter. Car racing anytime, when I was younger."

She wished he would give a direct answer to at least one of her questions. "Yes, but did you ever dream about the Olympics?"

Pulling himself from the pool, the prince came near. "It would have been pointless."

"Why?" she demanded. "Kristoffer competes, and his father's a prince."

"His father is healthy as an ox. Mine was never well," Jack said. "I had to handle any business that required travel and be prepared to take over at any time. Besides…" He broke off.

Kim barely squelched the urge to throw twigs at him. "Besides *what?*"

His mouth twitched. "I'm being evasive tonight, aren't I? Well, all right. If Kristoffer didn't keep himself busy diving, Igor might suspect his son of plotting to depose him."

"He would be suspicious of his own son?" Kim remembered the cold-eyed Zakovian prince and his theatrical entrance at his ball. "The man must live in a very dark world."

"I never thought of it that way, but you're right." Reaching out, Jack fluffed Kim's hair away from her temple. "I suppose some men live in terror that fate will take away their power and position."

"What would you do?" she asked. "If fate took it all back?"

In the silver light he stood silent for a while, not even shivering in the cool air. Then he said, "Run away with you."

She reached to touch his cheek and found it warm. The musky tang of his skin and the angled glint of his eyes combined to ignite her feminine instincts.

"Jack," she whispered.

"Not here," he said, and scooped her into his arms.

Kim's cheek pressed against his shoulder, relishing the dampness of his skin. Being held tight to his almost nude body, sharing the sheen of water left from the pond, felt startlingly intimate.

He strode down the path, each footfall reverberating through her marrow. She could hear Jack's heart beating, almost as fast as her own. Even the key hanging around his neck seemed like a promise of admittance to secret places.

They had reached an understanding without words. Tomorrow they would be transformed back into their ordinary selves, but tonight there was no need for promises and no thought of consequences.

Opening the French doors, Jack swept her into his bedchamber. As he paused to turn the lock, she glimpsed a room filled with carved furniture and heavy masculine fabrics.

A canopy sheltered the bed, and when he laid her on the silken coverlet, he drew the curtains to close them in. Filtered lamplight turned his skin to gold.

Kim had the sense that they had left the real world and entered a magical one that only Jack could conjure. The knowledge that all too soon it would vanish made her want him all the more.

Within their enclosure he arched over her, his mouth meeting hers as his hands cupped the eager softness of her breasts. A hunger beyond enchantment welled at every point in her body.

Her hands traced the classical perfection of his back, down to the narrow waist and the tight hardness of his haunches. At his probing her tongue met his, stroking and inviting.

He smoothed her gown upward until her waist and breasts lay naked for the claiming and eased away her panties. With a long sigh, Kim allowed him to explore and cover her, relishing the rugged feel of his skin against hers.

Slowly he tasted her throat, then drew her hands above her head. The movement pressed her breasts upward, the taut nipples pointed toward him, her vulnerable core ready.

But her sorceror wanted to enjoy his willing captive. He claimed each mound in turn, teasing it with his lips, then brushing her quivering stomach. Only when she gasped, barely able to bear the exquisite agony, did she feel Jack's hips slide atop hers.

There were no words and no need for them. Their mouths met and he penetrated her with his tongue and his powerful wand at the same time.

Pleasure and a deep ache rioted through Kim. She arched against him, moving eagerly along his shaft.

His grip on her wrists tightened as he reasserted his magic spell. It surprised her that a man could possess such control, holding back as he tantalized her, drawing away and then thrusting into her again.

She needed him as she needed air to breathe. Eager to drive his passions beyond the brink, Kim rubbed her hips against his in a bewitching rhythm of her own. His ragged gasp proved her charm was working.

A groan marked the tearing away of boundaries. For once in his life, the prince lost control. His hands released her wrists and braced against the bed as he deepened his strokes.

Kim had never known a man and woman could take each other with such tender force. There seemed no end and she wanted none, only to be plundered again and again by this conquering monarch and to conquer him in turn.

With a volcanic convulsion, their passion burst. Heat rocketed as their bodies vibrated together. She felt his excitement and fulfillment and knew he felt hers, as if they were one being.

For a precious moment, Jack continued moving inside her, and then he sank beside Kim with a sigh of infinite contentment. The fire he'd lit smoldered on inside her, giving promise of future conflagrations.

THE MAGNIFICENT RELEASE of weeks of pent-up passion left Jack with a pleasurable buzz in every muscle and nerve. He hoped Kim had experienced the same joy, something to treasure long after she regained her freedom and returned to the life she cherished.

From the moment she touched him beside the pool, he had lost all sense of restraint. She possessed the power to strip away years of self-control and release his deepest emotions.

Now, somehow, he must gather them up again. He had maneuvered and manipulated Kim, and despite that she had given him this precious gift. He had no right to make any further demands on her.

Then a realization of what they had done, or might

have done, dashed away his languor. Jack sat up sharply.

Kim stirred beside him. "What's wrong?"

He searched for diplomatic phrasing and found none. "What if you're pregnant?"

"I should think you'd be pleased."

He had expected her to be more upset at the prospect. "From a selfish perspective, I would be. But you never agreed—that is, it would be dishonorable to trick you into bearing me an heir."

"You didn't trick me." She stretched sleepily. "I'm a consenting adult, you know."

Once, Jack would have agreed and even congratulated himself on achieving his goal so easily. He had lured his princess to Lindelor and perhaps gotten her with child, and she didn't even seem angry about it.

But he could not bear to take advantage of Kim. Eventually, his dishonesty would destroy the trust between them. "Nevertheless, I haven't been completely truthful."

"You mean, you aren't really the prince?" she teased.

The response startled a small chuckle from him, but his amusement faded quickly. "I didn't mean about that. But—"

"Oh, Jack!" In the glow of filtered light, he caught the mischievous curve of her lips. "Stop torturing yourself. I doubt very much that I'm pregnant. It's the wrong time of the month."

"Thank God," he said, and flopped back on the pillow.

Kim regarded him in astonishment. "Are you that eager to get rid of me?"

"Get rid of you?" he said. "Of course not."

"Then what's going on?"

He had to tell her. He had tried earlier that evening, but had let himself get distracted. For heaven's sake, he wasn't turning into a coward, was he? "It's about the million dollars."

"Excuse me?" said Kim.

"I never gave it to you."

The silence lengthened. She sat frozen, still wearing a half smile. Her nightgown had slid over her breasts, but her slim legs were invitingly bared. Jack wondered if she would ever let him touch her again.

"You didn't?" she said at last.

"We had agreed that I would give you a cashier's check after the ceremony," Jack said. "I was going to give it to you that night, when we were alone."

"Then I got knocked on the head."

"And conveniently forgot, and I could see that if I told the truth you would immediately get an annulment," he continued, letting the words spill out. There was something addictive about confession. "What did you need it for, anyway?"

"My father," she said dully. "To save my father's business. Without his knowing, of course."

That made Jack feel even worse. "I'm sure something can be arranged. You were talking earlier about Lindelor manufacturing its own microcomputers. Perhaps we could make him a partner and take advantage of his expertise. Or we might buy shares in his company, purely as a good investment. We could use a connection in the computer field."

"That would be nice." Kim sounded as if she were operating on automatic pilot.

"Aren't you going to do something?" Jack asked. "Such as hit me with a pillow?"

"A pillow isn't hard enough." At least she was showing a hint of emotion.

"How about a rock?"

"You're the prince. I'd be arrested."

"Go ahead, slug me," he said with a trace of hope. If she could get the rage out of her system, maybe they could start over.

But she only shook her head and swung out of bed. When she parted the curtains he felt as if an invisible barrier had been breached, letting in the cold air of reality.

SOMEHOW KIM GOT BACK to her room, removed her gown and took a long shower. As she slipped between the sheets, she felt as if she had left parts of herself distributed over every centimeter between her bed and Jack's.

What had happened between them tonight surpassed anything in her experience. They had possessed each other in every sense of the word.

And then he had sprung that bombshell. This entire time, while she'd been searching for the money, he'd been lying to her. She obviously couldn't stay married to a man who would use her so shamelessly.

Emotions jumbled in Kim's brain. She kept feeling the tender demands of his mouth and the power of his body inside hers. She ached with his imprint.

Again and again, she tried to find a way to forgive him. He'd been trying to save his country, hadn't he? And he'd been troubled by the possibility that she might become pregnant unintentionally—or at least he'd appeared to be.

How could she know what such a man was really thinking? He came from a different world. Since childhood, he'd been trained to hold the position of prince and to move in a sphere of international politics. To him, she might be merely a pawn. A desirable one, perhaps, but a pawn nevertheless.

The cruel truth was that she could no longer bring herself to trust him. At one level, she knew Jack would protect her with his life. He'd done that once already. But what he'd really been protecting was Lindelor's future.

If the treaty were nullified, her usefulness would end. True, the sizzling attraction between them would remain, but for how long?

In this world, Kim couldn't pretend to know the rules. Did the prince of Lindelor value fidelity and lifelong intimacy the way she did? Or did he consider a wife someone who stayed home and attended charity teas while the husband skied his way into one heart after another?

If she could have, she would have packed her clothes—just hers, not the ones Siegfried had purchased—and left tonight. But the threat from Zakovia still loomed over her.

She was going to have to carry out this charade for the next few days and hope the would-be assassins could be captured. Then she and Jack would both be free.

THE NEXT MORNING, Kim awoke with dry, scratchy eyes. She feared at first she might be catching a cold, but decided as she dressed that she was recuperating from jet lag.

The heaviness in her chest was less easily explained. All night she had found herself curling against empty space, missing the security of Jack's arms.

But it was a false security, she reminded herself as she selected a teal-green pantsuit, which was the closest thing to jeans she could locate in her wardrobe.

Lady Nanette appeared, seeming puzzled at finding Kim alone. Obviously, her departure with Jack from the reception had aroused expectations among the nobility.

She had to remember that they, too, were hoping for an heir. With uncharacteristic cynicism, Kim wondered if their friendliness the previous evening had been motivated solely by her role as royal incubator.

After Kim dressed, Lady Nanette guided her to a large glass-walled room set with small tables. A breakfast buffet waited at one side, and Kim could see that the other diners were nearly finished.

It felt odd to realize that all these people lived in the palace. What must it be like, never to have one's own kitchen?

Lovely, she decided as she piled her plate with fruit and eggs and a muffin. Just lovely.

Jack sat at a table with Pierre and Angela. Not wanting to make an open breach, Kim joined them.

The shadows beneath the prince's eyes testified that he, too, had had a restless night. But Angela, bouncing on the edge of her chair, didn't appear to notice.

"Most of the competitors arrive today," the brunette explained. "They'll be wanting to get settled and put in some practice before the competition starts tomorrow."

Pierre, who looked as if his teeth hurt, had mashed his sausage and potatoes into an unappetizing mess.

The prospect of seeing his arch rival again must be wreaking havoc with his appetite.

At the front of the room, Hans loudly tapped a pointer on a large easel, where he had set a poster board marked with the swimming-and-diving schedule. The foreign minister looked a bit haggard, and Kim wondered how her aunt was feeling today.

In matters of the heart, it would appear the men of Lindelor were not shining. But she couldn't muster a great deal of sympathy.

"People keep asking me for advance programs, but we've only printed enough for the ticket holders and competitors," Hans said as the hum of conversation subsided. "Instead, I thought I might explain the schedule to you now and review a few pertinent facts for those who are, uh, new to our ranks."

In the next few minutes Kim learned that the swim meet was the biennial Prince's Cup. A hundred-year-old tradition, it involved only male competitors. In the interest of fairness, a matching meet for women would be held the following month in Munich.

The meet would open and close at the outdoor pool, where the diving events were scheduled. The springboard competition would be first, followed by platform.

Simultaneously, swimming contests were scheduled indoors. Kim's mind glazed over at the mention of so many events: freestyles, backstrokes, breaststrokes and butterflies of various lengths, plus medleys and relays.

As Hans finished to polite applause, the ripple of conversation resumed, then died again as a small group of people entered through the far doors. Kim made out the open face and athletic figure of Grand Duke Kristoffer, with a woman on his arm.

The newcomer was tall and slim, with short salt-and-pepper hair. There was something familiar about her haughty features and watchful expression.

Another image jolted into Kim's mind. This time, the woman had long blond hair and was driving a car at Newport Center, the one that had nearly hit Kim and Hans. She'd been at the Zakovian ball as well, and she was the same height and build as the smaller of the two snowmobilers.

It would appear that one of the assassins had arrived. And she was leaning close to Kristoffer, smiling up at him.

Chapter Thirteen

"That rotten sneak!" Angela burst out when they were alone. The young woman had barely contained herself during the obligatory greetings to the Zakovians and had ignored Kristoffer's attempts to catch her eye. "He's a part of the plot! That scoundrel!"

Kim had wasted no time, as soon as the newcomers departed, in telling the Lindelorians who the woman was. Now she waited as Jack mulled over this information.

"I'm not surprised about the grand duke," said Pierre. "A dog will run with its own kind."

"I wouldn't be too quick to condemn him." Hans kept his voice low, as if they might be overheard, even though everyone else had left the breakfast room. "Gretchen Weil is an official of the Zakovian Swim Federation. He may not have had much choice about bringing her."

"Do you see any other divers with swim officials hanging on them?" demanded Angela.

"At least we know one of the players," murmured the prince. "But there must be more."

That was all he said. He continued to keep his plans for protecting Kim a secret, even from her.

The Hotel de Lindelor and the adjacent swim center, where she and Jack drove after breakfast, were filled with every conceivable shape and size of visitor. For a while Kim stared at everyone, searching for a glimpse of red hair or a stocky build, until she realized she was driving herself crazy.

Finally she concentrated on her official duty as princess, greeting competitors from China and Japan, Russia and France, Germany and Brazil. There was even a team from the United States. When one of the divers commented on how well Kim spoke English, it took considerable presence of mind not to blurt, "But I'm American!"

Was she? Certainly, she would be again as soon as the marriage ended, but that prospect failed to revive her spirits.

It was hard to read Jack's emotions. Schooled from an early age at holding himself in check, he revealed only the occasional twitch of a jaw muscle or gentle hand on Kim's elbow, guiding her. And even those might mean nothing.

Surely he hadn't put the night before out of his mind. He simply possessed more self-discipline than most men.

Kim wished they were alone so they could clear the air. Then she remembered how foolish it would be to rely on anything he said. His frankness might be assumed; his tenderness, manipulative. It was impossible to forget that he had been lying to her all along.

Besides, there were more important things to worry about. Such as whether an innocuous young swimmer might suddenly pull a knife or the gardener mowing the grass might attempt to run her down. When a car backfired, Kim's heart performed a tango in her throat.

However, she reminded herself, today's appearance hadn't been scheduled. It was far more likely an attack was planned for tomorrow.

"You're a real trooper," Jack said as they headed back to the palace to prepare for dinner. "I know it must be tedious, welcoming all those people, but you conducted yourself like a princess."

They were alone in the carriage except for Hans, who had fallen asleep the instant his head touched a cushion. Pierre had remained at the swim center, where he and Angela were assisting latecomers.

"Thanks, I guess." Kim gazed out the window at the cottages and shops. The streets were crowded with tourists in town for the Prince's Cup.

It was a scene out of some childhood fantasy, the flower-brightened cottages and the shopkeepers wearing traditional alpine costumes. With deep sadness, she realized that all her life she had felt she belonged in this place.

But she didn't really. She was no more Lindelorian than were those tourists buying postcards and tiny replicas of the country's flag.

"What does the wolf stand for, anyway?" she asked. "Is it from the Middle Ages?"

"Lindelor has been a distinct entity since around 1300, when Switzerland broke free of Austria, but we didn't have a flag back then," Jack said. "We were part of the Swiss Federation until 1515 when Greater Zakovia was formed, which included us."

The carriage rumbled over some uneven stones and Hans snorted in his sleep, then resumed his regular breathing.

I didn't know the two were once united," Kim said, intrigued.

"In 1803, the two ruling families quarreled over whether to remain neutral or join with Napoleon and the alliance was dissolved," Jack went on. "Lindelor stayed out of the war. Zakovia got involved and was defeated."

"A lesson it apparently didn't learn very well," Kim said, thinking of that country's disastrous involvement in World War II. "But where did the wolf come in?"

"At first our flag had a simple green background with a red cross in the upper left corner," Jack said. "Then, when Dr. Mitchell discovered the healing powers of our spas, he claimed it was because he saw a sick wolf crawling to the water and drinking. The animal stood up a few minutes later and walked away."

"So the wolf doesn't represent ferocity," Kim said. "It's a symbol of healing."

Impulsively, Jack took her hands in his. "I think it's time we tried a little healing of our own. Last night—"

The carriage rolled to a stop. Staring out the window, Kim realized they had reached the castle.

Beside her, the prince made a most unregal face. "Rotten timing."

Half of Kim's brain urged her to invite him back to her room and listen to what he had to say. The other half counseled caution.

There was no assurance the treaty could be dissolved, so he still had plenty to gain by wooing her. With effort, she forced herself to gaze into his pleading eyes and say, "Let's just leave things as they are, shall we?"

Reluctantly Jack released her. But the set of his mouth warned that he hadn't given up.

THE OPENING CEREMONIES were held at noon the following day. From the royal box atop the tiers of seating that flanked the outdoor pool, Jack delivered a short welcoming speech and released a huge bouquet of red, white and green balloons.

He watched them float upward, polka-dotting the sky. On this sunny day, with the air so clear that the mountains appeared carved from crystal, a sense of exhilaration bubbled through his bloodstream. One glance at Kim showed her face glowing with a delight that matched his own.

She was a part of this place. Why couldn't he make her see it?

To the cheers of the onlookers, Jack declared the games officially open. Just before he sat down, his gaze swept the crowd, watching for that one movement, that one flick of the eye that might signal an attack, but he saw nothing.

Kim's recognition of the female assassin had confirmed Jack's belief that another attempt would be made and that it would be made here. Igor hadn't given up. Perhaps he never would.

Since Kristoffer was not competing in the springboard event, he sat in the stands, accompanied by Gretchen. The grand duke wore a troubled expression. He kept trying to catch Angela's attention, but she sat in the royal box, stony faced beside Pierre.

Jack couldn't believe the grand duke was part of his father's scheming. For one thing, Kristoffer displayed his emotions so openly that he would be useless at any kind of skulduggery. For another thing, the man was too much in love with Angela to deliberately antagonize her.

After the first few rounds of compulsory dives, Jack realized it was time for him and the princess to move indoors. Courtesy required them to observe the swimming races before returning to the palace. After that they could attend whatever events they wished, or none at all until the closing ceremonies three days away.

The Zakovians would surely make an attempt on Kim in these open surroundings, where it was impossible to keep tabs on all the spectators and team hangers-on. Jack could only be watchful and hope that either he, his security agents or his backup plan would suffice.

He had never felt so vulnerable, even though he was surrounded by friends and family. In the reserved seating nearby, he could identify even from this angle the familiar figures of Lady Nanette and her husband, along with Aunt Rapunzel. Angela's mother, Lady Schnappsenfeld, a woman so reclusive she was almost a hermit, sat decorously in place, as did Hans's taciturn father and peppery stepmother, the Baron and Baroness Frick.

"Your Highness?" Pierre leaned across the box. "I believe the fifty-meter freestyle is about to begin indoors."

"Thank you." Jack waited until a British competitor had completed his dive, then whispered in Kim's ear and they both made a quick escape.

This was the most dangerous part, moving from one spot to another. Plainclothes security agents were fanning out along each of several possible routes, but there were too many variables for Jack's taste.

He chose not to take Kim outside along the sidewalk, which would lead them past a welter of cars and buses. It would be easy for a cyclist or skateboarder to dart toward them.

He could feel Kim's tension as he escorted her by the back route, into the building that housed the locker rooms. The urge to reassure her was strong, but he must put all his energy into keeping alert.

Whenever he focused on Kim, the rest of the world tended to vanish from his mind. Even now, her nearness tingled through his senses.

Flares of heat along his nerve endings reminded him of their intense passion, an experience beyond anything Jack had known before. The night before had been agony, when he'd forced himself to leave her alone until there was time to reestablish their closeness. But first he had to keep her alive.

With quick steps, he steered Kim along a serpentine course toward the indoor pool. A maze of passageways provided access to locker rooms, showers, weight facilities, whirlpool baths and a clinic to treat the inevitable sprains and bruises.

With every footstep, Jack heard echoes that seemed to come from distant passageways. Voices resounded from the depths of the building, making it impossible to define which noises originated close by.

Among the pervasive scents of chlorine and men's aftershave, he caught a whiff of something medicinal. Kim noticed it, too. "Why does it smell like a doctor's office?"

"We're near the clinic," Jack said. "Unless that's some new antiseptic cleanser."

Ahead of them, an ordinary-looking couple who were actually security agents rounded a corner and disappeared. Pierre and Angela, who had been bringing up the rear, had been hailed by an Austrian diver, an old friend of Pierre's, and Jack realized with a start that they must have dropped behind.

He and Kim were momentarily unguarded. It was exactly the kind of situation he had wanted to prevent.

To the left, they were passing an unmarked door that probably led to a custodial closet. To the right down a side corridor, Jack glimpsed something white like a doctor's coat, coming out of a room.

The door to the closet flew open. In that heart-stopping moment, Jack realized that his trap for the Zakovians had turned into a trap for him and his wife.

"Run!" He started to push Kim forward, and then something blunt came crashing down on his head.

AS THE CLOSET DOOR smashed open, a dark figure leaped out, wielding a club and blocking the path. A scream stuck in Kim's throat as she dodged to the right, but Jack wasn't quick enough.

She saw him go down and she ached to stop and help, but the attacker was hefting his club to take a swing at her. Adrenaline pounding through her arteries, Kim turned and ran.

Her skirt and heels hampered her speed and she stumbled. But there were no footsteps behind her. The attacker must have given up, but why?

Ahead of her, a man in a white coat was coming out of the clinic. "Are you a doctor?" she demanded. "The prince is hurt! You have to help—"

Then she saw the man's face. Although his hair had been bleached nearly white, there was no mistaking the truck driver who had been changing a tire near her doctor's office. He had the same round, freckled face and impatient sneer.

In his hand loomed a syringe that, to Kim, looked big enough to inject a horse.

Blind fury replaced her terror. Who did this jerk think he was dealing with, anyway, some wimpy princess raised in an ivory tower?

From her skirt pocket, she whipped a can of pepper spray and shot the man right in the eyes. With a shriek, he stumbled backward, giving Kim a chance to plant a kick where it would hurt most.

The syringe clattered to the floor. She jumped on it with both feet and a pungent smell filled the air.

Hearing a shout behind her, Kim swung around. Pierre and the Austrian diver were pelting toward her while Angela knelt over Jack.

"Where'd he go?" Kim demanded. "The other guy?"

Pierre shook his head. "We didn't see anyone. Are you all right?"

As she nodded, others materialized, including the security couple who had been walking ahead of them. In minutes, the ersatz doctor was bound and carted off, while Jack was carried on a gurney toward the clinic.

Already he was coming around, asking for her. She caught his hand as the cart went by. "I'm fine. We California girls come prepared."

The prince managed a weak smile. There was a lump on the side of his head.

"At least I haven't lost my memory," he said. "I still remember where I put the million dollars."

The joke startled a laugh from Kim, and her heart

gave a lurch. How could she ever bear to lose this man?

While Pierre gave orders to track the escaped villain and try to recover a sample of the spilled poison, the physician in charge examined the prince and pronounced him likely to develop a severe headache but nothing worse.

"He'll have to be watched for signs of a concussion, but right now I'm not seeing anything," the doctor said. "I'd recommend we keep him overnight in the hospital."

Kim shook her head. "He's too vulnerable. I want him back at the palace."

In a sense, she supposed she had no right to make such decisions for Jack, but he was too woozy to think clearly. And who could decide better what was in his best interest than the woman who loved him?

The realization stung, but she refused to dwell on it. All right, so she loved him, while she had no idea how he really felt about her. It didn't matter. She was strong enough to survive, come what may.

A woman who could fell an assassin with pepper spray could certainly overcome a broken heart.

JACK'S EYES FLICKERED open, but the throbbing in his head made him wish he were still asleep.

He lay in his own bed, among the familiar scents of laundry soap and aftershave. The sheets felt crisp and freshly ironed, a tribute to Siegfried's unflagging dedication.

Through the translucent curtains he could see a woman sitting in a chair. Brushing aside the draperies he smiled as he caught a glimpse of Kim. She had dozed off curled in an armchair, a book on her lap.

Lamplight brought out the reddish highlights of her hair. Her embroidered caftan had slipped low on one shoulder, revealing the exquisite fineness of her bones.

Thank heaven she was safe. Jack's stomach clenched at realizing how close he had come to losing her. All his backup plans had gone for nothing. Even on his home territory, among friends, Kim would have been killed if not for her own resourcefulness.

He would risk his own life a thousand times for the good of his country, but he had no right to take such chances with Kim's.

She stirred, knocking her book to the floor with a thump. After a dazed moment, her eyes met his. "Oh! You're up! Well, in a manner of speaking."

Jack nodded, and wished he hadn't.

"Your head!" Picking up the book and setting it aside, Kim got to her feet. "The doctor left some pain pills."

"Will they make me woozy? Then I'll wait."

Pulling the curtains open wider, she sat on the edge of the bed. Her slim figure made only a slight indentation, but her vitality filled the canopied space. "The man they caught, the one who used to have red hair, he has Swiss citizenship and no one at the swim meet admits to knowing him. He doesn't seem to have any direct links to Prince Igor."

"So we can't prove the Zakovians were behind the assassination attempt?" Jack had guessed as much. Igor wouldn't be stupid enough to implicate himself. "Did they find out what was in that syringe?"

"There wasn't enough left on the floor to test," Kim admitted. "Hans says it was probably something to induce a heart attack."

Jack pulled himself up and was pleased when Kim leaned forward to plump the pillows. He inhaled the perfume of her hair and wondered how, despite his injuries, his body could react with such masculine fervor.

It was in this very bed, two nights earlier, that they'd made love. He wanted desperately to pull her down beside him now, to hold her close and feel her warmth. But they had important matters to discuss.

"Kim," he said. "We have to dissolve the marriage now and send you home. I can only hope Igor won't pursue you once you're single."

She bit her lip. "We can't rely on that, Jack. Hans got a fax from Ladislaw in Los Angeles. He learned that Igor is in danger of defaulting on a large loan from a Middle Eastern oil emirate. He needs security for a new loan—like the assurance of future revenues from Lindelor. That means he has to kill me, and as soon as possible. I don't think we have any choice. We have to prove what he's doing, so you can dissolve the treaty."

"You mean go on trying to set a trap?" His voice grew hoarse with dismay. "I refuse to use you as bait one moment longer."

"Quite right," came a female voice from the doorway. Alarm pounded through Jack. How had the intruder gotten past the guards? "It's time I stopped acting like a selfish child."

The woman stepped into the light. Angela. No wonder he hadn't recognized her voice; he'd never heard her speak in such low, measured tones before or seen such a grim expression on her face.

She made an apologetic gesture. "My injuries— I've recovered better than I told you. I can have children. I only thought you would be happier with someone else, and so would I.''

Moisture glittered in Kim's eyes. "You're saying you would marry Jack?"

Angela shrugged. "We don't love each other, not the way you two do."

"But—" Kim stopped in confusion.

"Obviously, there are issues between you that can't be resolved," Angela went on. "I can understand that. This isn't your country and you haven't grown up as royalty."

Apparently his cousin had given up hope of marrying Kristoffer. And she was right, Jack thought; a union between the two of them made more sense than any other course.

He loved Kim as he could never love anyone else. He would miss her every day and every night of his life. But if it meant preserving her safety, he must make the sacrifice.

"But then you'll be in danger," Kim was pointing out.

"Perhaps I was, all the time," Angela said. "Take my accident, for example. I've wondered time and again why the pavement was so slick, as if it had been oiled."

Inwardly, Jack cursed himself for failing to see what should have been obvious to a man responsible for his country's security. "Why didn't you say something?"

"I suppose I didn't want to believe it," she admitted. "Kristoffer was there, don't you recall? I didn't want to believe he would do such a thing. But who else could it have been?"

Perhaps some Zakovian agent, Jack thought. But

there was no point in making excuses for the grand duke, when Angela had surely considered all possibilities before coming here tonight.

"Would you mind waiting until the closing ceremonies to announce the news?" Angela went on. "A lot of my friends have come into town for the competition. I should like to be free to party without worrying that someone will shove a poisoned needle in my arm."

"Of course." Jack glanced at Kim. She had wrapped her arms around herself, as if to hold her feelings inside.

Finally, she said, "Thanks, Angela. That took a lot of courage."

"Not so much." His cousin reached out and patted Kim's shoulder. "It's my country I'm saving, you know."

After she left, Jack took Kim's hands in his and sat watching her. He kept trying to think of a poetic way to express his feelings but found none. "The important thing is to keep you safe."

The color had drained from her cheeks. "Is it?"

On the point of telling her how much he loved her and how much he wanted her to stay, he stopped himself harshly. He must seize this chance to free her from Igor's machinations. "Yes. You should go home and live your own life."

Her mouth twisted. "That's all you have to say?"

Also that I love you so much I can hardly breathe when I think of losing you. But how could he lure her into staying, purely for his own selfish happiness?

"Go home, Kim." The words came out raggedly, torn from his soul. "I'm only sorry I dragged you into this mess in the first place."

She sat for a moment longer, as if reluctant to pull her hands away. Then slowly she stood and walked into the shadows.

Chapter Fourteen

Kim spent the next two days in a daze. By rote, she greeted official visitors to the palace and took her place at meals beside Jack, who was recovering rapidly.

Inside, a dead weight swung where her heart used to be. She ought to feel relieved that the crushing danger was about to end. But all she experienced was the knife-edge of longing to see love burning in Jack's eyes and hear him beg her to stay.

Angela, on the other hand, flung herself into the festivities with a vengeance. Each morning she wafted from the palace in a swarm of friends and hangers-on. Several times a day she buzzed back to change clothes and tell Kim and Jack about the latest victories and losses.

Before it was even shown on TV Lindelor, they learned that a French swimmer had won the hundred-meter butterfly and an American had narrowly bested a German in the two-hundred-meter individual medley.

A Chinese diver conquered the springboard competition with a respectable but unspectacular 620.34 points. And, on the next-to-last day of the event,

Grand Duke Kristoffer of Zakovia took a narrow lead in the preliminary round of platform diving.

Through it all, Jack spent much time closeted with Hans. Occasionally the two of them drove to the swim meet, not to watch but to check on security arrangements for the final day.

The picturesque carriage was abandoned in favor of a bulletproof car, loaned by an industrial magnate in Italy who had bought it to discourage kidnappers. Security measures were tightened in the locker rooms, with metal detectors installed and participants' badges checked and rechecked.

Kim knew she ought to be eagerly anticipating the closing ceremonies, when Jack would announce their pending divorce and his engagement to Angela. She tried to imagine how pleasant it would be when she could once again travel without fear.

Instead, she kept picturing Jack as he emerged from the pool, silver in the moonlight. His teasing smile flashed through her dreams and she felt his body pressed against hers.

She tried to distance herself, to imagine herself remembering this castle and this country from the sunwashed reality of Southern California. Surely it would all appear as a dream.

But it was her home in Laguna Beach that struck her now as unreal. Was it possible she would no longer gaze from her window into a garden and never again share breakfast with Jack? She wouldn't even be around long enough to see that nasty bruise on his temple fade away.

As Kim went about her daily routine, Lady Nanette observed her with a troubled expression but never pried. The Lindelorian dislike of gossip was a distinct blessing.

The only relief came during Kim's brief calls home. At her suggestion her father had contacted Ladislaw at the trade mission and the two were drawing up a proposed partnership to build and program microcomputers for prosthetic devices.

As for Valerie, she admitted she and Hans had been indulging in hour-long telephone conversations. "I really miss him," she admitted. "The only problem is that I can't give up my work and he can't give up his."

Kim hoped there would be a happy ending for her aunt, if not for her.

On the final day of the competition, she awoke with a sense of dismay. No one knew about Jack's plans to marry Angela yet and so no formal plans had been made to expedite the divorce. But in her top drawer lay a ticket back to Los Angeles, bearing tomorrow's date.

Showering beneath a stream of hot water, she considered for the umpteenth time whether she should refuse the divorce and stay here, danger or not. But Jack himself had urged her to go.

If only it were possible to see into his heart! Silently, Kim admitted that if he really loved her she would stay without hesitation. But until the situation with Zakovia was resolved, she wasn't sure even Jack could separate his feelings for her from his loyalty to his country.

She emerged from the shower in a steam of indecision. Whatever might happen today, she didn't feel ready for it.

For the closing ceremonies she needed to wear

something princesslike, Kim decided as she surveyed the contents of her armoire. Not a ball gown, though—that would look ridiculous at a swim meet.

With a twinge of regret, she rejected an embroidered dirndl in the Lindelorian style. It would look painfully amiss when Jack announced that she was returning to America.

She settled on a midcalf-length skirt with a matching jacket made of soft, creamy fabric trimmed in green, with a green blouse to match. Studying the effect in the mirror, Kim noticed how bright her eyes looked today, as if filled with unshed tears.

Squaring her shoulders, she turned to face Lady Nanette, who had come to help with her hair. After tomorrow, she reflected, the lady-in-waiting would wait no more. Once again, Kim would be free to lounge around in jeans, to stick a cap on top of her unruly hair and dab on nothing more than lipstick as she ran to have lunch with Aunt Valerie.

She tried to pretend that she was looking forward to it.

JACK WAITED IN THE front hall, beneath a thirty-foot ceiling painted with angels, hunters, goatherds and wolves. As a child, he had found it endlessly fascinating. As a teenager, he had thought it garish. Now, as a man, he found it paled before the critical events about to take place in real life.

He had been pacing the palace for the past hour, buttoned and belted into his uniform. The polished black boots clicked over wooden floors and marble ones until it seemed he must surely be wearing a path.

Fortunately for his nerves, the palace was virtually empty. Everyone but the guards and staff had gone to watch the last day of competition. Jack regretted missing the events this year, but except for the diving finals right before the closing ceremonies he couldn't justify the risk to Kim.

The hardest thing he'd ever done had been to accept her airline ticket from Hans and carry it to her room. She'd taken it without a word, but he'd seen the pain in her expression.

Jack braced himself for what lay ahead. He was going to protect Kim for her own good. It was better to prevent the trap from being sprung than to risk turning her into a target.

It was too dangerous even to allow her to come with him today. He hadn't wanted to leave her behind in the palace, not when he and all his other officials were scheduled to be at the swim center. But a last-minute change of plans might foil the assassins.

His jaw tightening with resolve, Jack turned to watch as Kim and Lady Nanette approached, followed by a guard. Despite her elegant suit and the determined way she strode forward, there was something about the tentative curve of his wife's shoulders that revealed her vulnerability.

He wanted to tell her how lovely she looked with her hair a brilliant halo and her emerald eyes glimmering. Instead, he said, "I've decided you would be safer staying here."

Her chin came up. "Don't be ridiculous. I want to watch Kristoffer compete."

"You can see him on TV tonight."

"And I want to say goodbye to the people of Lindelor," Kim said. "I don't intend to sneak away as if I didn't care."

She possessed all the right instincts for a princess,

but in this case she had to back down. "You know Igor is planning to kill you."

"If I don't come, people might think I object to your plans to marry Angela," Kim persisted.

"You can give a TV interview tonight." Jack couldn't let her win this time, his stubborn, courageous wife. She was taking too big a risk.

"And—" She hesitated.

"What?" The word came out in a murmur, close to her ear. Jack wanted to keep this conversation private, even from someone he trusted as implicitly as Lady Nanette.

Kim's cheek brushed his, a sensual movement that made his breath come more quickly. "It's not enough for me to be free. You have to be free, too."

He lifted his head to regard her quizzically. "What does that mean?"

"I don't know what path you would choose if the treaty were dissolved." A tremulous undertone belied her air of calm. "I'm not sure you know, either. I want you to have that choice, which means we have to catch the killers. If I don't go, I doubt we ever will."

If he had a choice, Jack thought sharply, he would keep Kim with him forever. But she had made it clear long ago that she would never abandon her career to live as a princess.

"Kim—" he began, when Hans entered from a side corridor.

"They've begun the competition, Your Highness," said the foreign minister, who wore the green-and-white uniform he had earned as a major in the Lindelorian reserve army. "If we don't hurry, we'll miss the diving."

Jack knew he ought to insist that Kim stay behind, but he couldn't. He wanted every possible moment with her, as long as possible. And she'd made it clear that she wanted to come.

"Let's go, then," he said.

THEY RODE TO THE swim center in the armored car, with Lady Nanette sitting in the back and Jack driving. Today, he didn't even want to rely on a chauffeur.

To Kim's amazement, Hans had chosen to escort them on a motorcycle. He wore a gun strapped to his shoulder holster and kept a sharp eye open for attackers.

Other reserve officers, also in uniform, guarded the route to the swim center. The sight of them chilled Kim. In her dismay at Jack's sudden change of plans, she'd pushed aside her fears, but now they rushed back full force.

She must be crazy. What was she doing here anyway, pretending to be a Lindelorian princess when she was nothing but a title rep from Southern California? What did she know about international intrigue and dissolving treaties?

Kim glanced sidelong at Jack. He sat erect in his scarlet coat, hands clamped on the wheel and gaze raking the road with military precision. There were so many aspects to him, she wondered if it would ever be possible to know them all.

They pulled past the swim center and stopped at a side entrance. Soldiers rushed to open the car door.

Jack stayed close to Kim, his body sheltering hers as they hurried through a twisting corridor inside the building and emerged beside the spectators' stands at the outdoor pool. She could hardly see anything but a blur, they were moving so quickly.

Kim began to wish she hadn't come, but it was too late to back down now. Somehow she'd pictured a relaxed scene once they reached their destination, but although Jack obviously didn't want to disrupt the competition, he also had no intention of making her an easy target.

They approached the royal box via a circuitous route that forced several dozen spectators to stand and let them pass. On their faces, however, Kim saw only friendliness and sympathy.

When they sat, they were below and to one side of the box rather than inside it. Nearby were Hans, Pierre, Angela, Lady Nanette and other relatives from the palace.

Kim tried to focus on the competitors, who were completing the fifth in a series of six dives. According to the scoreboard, Kristoffer was in second place behind a French diver.

As she watched a Chinese entrant climb from the pool, her thoughts flew to how Jack had looked when he emerged from the palace pool and swept her into his arms. If only he would carry her to his bedroom, just one more time.

But now he wasn't even looking at her. His gaze darted across the stands, searching for any wayward motion.

The French diver arched off the platform, more than three stories above the water. He moved so fast, Kim couldn't count the twists and somersaults. She heard cheers as the young man slipped into the water with scarcely a ripple.

"Perfect!" said Angela. "I hope he wins." But she didn't sound excited by the prospect.

An Austrian diver was next, the one who had stopped Pierre and Angela the previous day. He completed a difficult backward dive, but raised a large splash when he landed.

Kristoffer came last, pausing atop the platform to gaze down at them. His eyes rested on Angela with a note of pleading, but the Lindelorian woman refused to acknowledge him.

Then he leaped off the board, executing a perfect one and a half somersault with a double twist and slipping into the water with ease. When his score came up, it put him in a tie with the French diver.

"Darn," said Angela.

In the lower stands Gretchen Weil, the woman with salt-and-pepper hair, sat alone. She appeared to be intent on the competition.

Was she watching for a signal from Kristoffer? Or was the plan to wait until the closing ceremonies?

Jack had instructed the previous night that as soon as he made the announcement that he was divorcing Kim, she was to depart. He wanted her well away from the stands before he broke the news about Angela, making it unlikely the assassins could catch the two women together. At that point, they would surely realize there was no point in eliminating one potential mother of princes without the other.

And then I go quietly home, and try to forget all this ever happened.

Kim closed her eyes, picturing herself driving along the freeway toward one of the real-estate offices where she sold title insurance. From the car radio boomed a traffic report, updated every ten minutes. A massive traffic jam on the 405. An accident on Interstate 5. Already, her blood pressure started to rise.

Seven of the divers had completed their final attempts. All lagged behind the three leaders, the men from France, Austria and Zakovia.

The Frenchman pulled off a difficult twisting dive and scored well. Kristoffer would have to be near perfection to beat him, but by now Kim had seen that the grand duke was capable of it.

The next-to-last competitor, from Austria, went next. He pulled out of his last somersault too low and landed a resounding belly flop. Murmurs of sympathy arose from the onlookers, but the man swam quickly toward the edge, uninjured.

Everyone's gaze riveted on Kristoffer, emerging atop the platform. Even Jack was caught up in the excitement.

With a start, Kim realized the danger might come right here and right now. This was the moment when people's attention was distracted.

But she saw nothing amiss, no one heading toward her, no one turning in the stands. Even Gretchen Weil was staring at the water.

Then Kim realized that although the Austrian diver had vanished, she hadn't seen him leave the pool. He didn't appear to be anywhere around.

He must have submerged, but why? If he was hurt, wouldn't he be floating? No one else appeared to have noticed the man's disappearance as Kristoffer got into position for his dive.

All eyes were focused at the top of the platform. All eyes, that was, except for Kim's. She seemed to be the only one aware that a dark head had surfaced directly in front of her, and from the water he was lifting a small dart gun.

It had been secured beneath the waterline. Of course!

A scream caught in her throat. She couldn't believe that fear would paralyze her vocal cords, but at this moment she could hardly breathe, let alone shout.

Her hand clamped on to Jack's arm, but he didn't respond. Around them, everyone was squirming with anticipation. He must be assuming she was just on edge like the others.

Say something, do something, fall down, groan, anything! But she was crammed in here, wedged between bodies with nowhere to go. All she could do was lean to one side, but that was enough. A dart hissed by and vanished into empty space behind her.

The only one who seemed to notice her sudden movement was Kristoffer, high above the pool. Kim saw shock and disbelief flash across his face.

Beside her, Jack started to turn to see why she'd shifted position, but he wasn't alarmed yet—just curious. And down in the pool the Austrian raised his gun to take another shot.

Kristoffer went off the board, not in a smooth, calculated dive but as a human cannonball, hurtling directly toward the would-be assassin. A confused gasp went up from the crowd.

"Help!" The word gasped from Kim's mouth and finally Jack spotted the man in the water and pulled her roughly behind him, his body shielding hers.

In the instant before he covered her, she witnessed the Austrian disappearing beneath Kristoffer and the second dart falling harmlessly onto the concrete.

A moment later, emerging from behind Jack, Kim

saw guards running toward the water and pandemonium erupting around her. People started from their seats and the other divers crowded forward.

"It may not be over," the prince said grimly. "Kim, stay down!"

"Gretchen!" She pointed along the stands. "Where'd she go?" The Zakovian official's seat was empty.

"Damn!" Jack turned to survey the stands, but it was too late. The woman with salt-and-pepper hair and the coldest gaze Kim had ever seen had taken advantage of the confusion to slip into place beside them. In her hand sparkled a bejeweled pin, its sharp point thrusting toward Kim's arm.

JACK COULDN'T MOVE quickly enough. All the forces of gravity and inertia seemed to drag him into slow motion as he lunged across Kim, trying to intercept the poisoned pin. But he was in the wrong position, at the wrong angle.

Then miraculously the Zakovian woman shuddered. Just as he registered the crack of a small-caliber gun, the brooch fell from her numb fingers and the woman collapsed.

In the seat below, Aunt Rapunzel gave a nod of satisfaction and replaced her pearl-encrusted gun in her purse. To her left, Lady Nanette sighed with disappointment at not having been fast enough, and put away her own gun. To the right, Angela's mother, Lady Schnappsenfeld, continued to wield her small weapon for a few more precautionary seconds.

The women of Lindelor, trained in weaponry and national defense alongside the men since the days of

World War II, had validated Jack's trust in them as the ultimate backup plan.

He took an unsteady breath, shaken by how near he had come to losing everything that mattered. His arms closed around Kim and he held her close, trying to still her trembling.

"I'm sorry," he said. "I never thought they would get this far."

The worst part was that both times he had been powerless to save her. The fact that his own planning had paid off eased Jack's guilt a little, but not enough.

Below, guards were handcuffing the Austrian diver under Hans's supervision, but from the way the prisoner lay groaning on the concrete, it didn't look as if he would be making any escape attempts. Assisted from the water, Kristoffer sank to the ground nearby.

With a jolt, Jack realized that the grand duke had been injured while saving Kim's life. As prince of Lindelor, Jack owed the man every possible assistance.

His attention was drawn away as security agents and a couple of medics came to take charge of Gretchen's body. At the same time, Pierre and Angela approached.

"Your Highness, I'd suggest we get the princess back to the palace right away," said the private secretary. "Heaven knows what other booby traps they've laid."

Jack gave reluctant consent. He would have preferred to keep Kim nearby, but her coloring had gone ashen. Besides, Pierre was right.

"I shall stay with her," Angela volunteered.

By the pool, Kristoffer sat up, waving to show he was all right. Well, not entirely all right. When the grand duke attempted to stand, he immediately sank down, his right leg unable to hold his weight.

"I hate to say it, but maybe you should give our Zakovian friend some moral support," Pierre told Angela as he offered Kim his arm.

"Don't be ridiculous," she retorted. "The princess is the one who needs moral support. Besides, Jack *has* to stay. I'm sure he'll take fine care of the grand duke." From her edgy tone, apparently she still hadn't forgiven her former boyfriend for squiring Gretchen.

About to suggest that Lady Nanette could go with Kim, Jack realized the lady-in-waiting had left her seat. People were milling through the stands and cramming into the pool area, and he couldn't spot her in the crush.

"She's right," he said. "Kim needs someone to look after her, and you'll be busy driving." Pierre didn't look happy about it, but he nodded.

A short time later, as Jack watched the three of them drive away together with a guard following on a motorcycle, he felt a quiver of unease. He should have kept Kim with him.

Well, he couldn't call them back now without making a scene. The important thing was that they were both safe, he reflected as he hurried back to make sure Kristoffer's injuries were nothing worse than a broken leg.

KIM LEANED AGAINST the cushions, too overwhelmed by the events of the past few minutes to enjoy the sights of the town as she usually did. Twice she'd thought she was going to die. She wondered if the pounding of her heart would ever abate.

One thing was for sure. Those images—the diver in the water, the Zakovian woman leaning toward her—had been stamped into her brain forever.

She kept seeing Gretchen's cold eyes, so eerily familiar. Of course, Kim had observed her several times before, behind the wheel of a car and at the Zakovian ball. But they hadn't been close enough for a good look, and yet Kim had instantly recognized the frigid pale-blue irises with their unusual specks of brown.

"I can hardly believe it," Angela was saying beside her. "That Austrian diver was just chatting us up the other day. He must have stopped us on purpose to distract us! Friedrich, that's his name, or at least that's what he said. He's probably got false papers, don't you think?"

"I'm going to take an alternate route," Pierre announced from the front seat. "I think we should make ourselves as difficult a target as possible."

"You don't think they'll make another attempt, do you?" Angela asked, horrified.

Kim wondered if the Lindelorian woman was having second thoughts about becoming princess. After today, it appeared to be an even more high-risk job than she'd bargained for.

"I don't think we can take anything for granted," said Pierre.

Why do I keep seeing those eyes?

Then she realized why they looked familiar. Gretchen had been at the hotel in Los Angeles. The memory was finally returning.

Kim could see them in a kind of three-dimensional snapshot, the red-haired man and the blond woman. They were stalking toward her, but there was something strange about the setting.

Steel counters. Steel sinks. The smell of onions.

The pair had attacked her in the hotel kitchen. But she'd been heading for the ladies' room. How had she gotten so far off course?

"You certainly are taking the scenic route," Angela observed.

Terror clamped across Kim's chest. Her body seemed to recognize danger a moment before her brain could put the last puzzle piece into place.

Pierre. He was the one who had given her false directions at the hotel, sending her to the kitchen instead of the bathroom. He must be the Zakovians' inside contact.

And now, accompanied by a guard who was probably another infiltrator, they were speeding out of town without so much as a pistol-wielding old lady to protect them.

Chapter Fifteen

By the time Jack returned to the pool, he found that Kristoffer had been removed to the clinic for an X ray. In Jack's eagerness to check on the grand duke, he waved aside Hans's urging that he grant a few minutes to TV Lindelor.

"I'll give an interview later," Jack instructed.

"What about the closing ceremonies?" asked the foreign minister, dutiful as always.

"Ask everyone to wait, please." With that, Jack hurried to the clinic.

He arrived just as Kristoffer was wheeled back from his X ray. "Nice, clean break," the grand duke announced cheerily. "How's my target?"

"Numerous fractures and abrasions," said the doctor. "They've taken him to the hospital under guard."

"He'll have plenty of time to heal," Jack growled. "Twenty or thirty years, I hope."

"I couldn't believe it when I saw him aiming at Kim." The duke stopped to stare at a draped figure on a gurney. "Who is that?"

With dismay, Jack realized this was a harsh way to let the Zakovian heir know that his former companion was dead. Although he didn't believe there was any romantic attachment between Kristoffer and Gretchen, he had to assume they were at least friends.

He spoke quietly to the doctor, who immediately summoned an orderly to remove the body. Then Jack turned to Kristoffer. "It's Ms. Weil. I'm sorry."

"I'm not." The diver propped himself on his elbows. "My father ordered me to bring her, on threat of disinheriting me. Can you believe that? I knew she must be a spy. But—did she try to kill Kim, too?"

"She tried to stab her," Jack said. "With a pin. We assume it was poisoned."

"Thank God you stopped her."

"Actually, it was Aunt Rapunzel who shot her."

The grand duke quirked an eyebrow. "Give the lady my respects."

The man's cavalier attitude might be a sign of emotional shock, Jack supposed. "I'm afraid your father's not going to be happy with you for foiling his scheme."

Kristoffer shrugged. "Using me to plant an assassin has dishonored us both. I never would have brought her if I'd realized what he intended. I doubt our people will take it kindly, either. If you'll allow TV Lindelor to interview me, we could broadcast my statement calling for his removal."

"I'll help in any way I can." Jack caught his breath. To have the grand duke take Lindelor's side would be a tremendous boon, but there was one more vital issue at stake. "Also, I must inform you that I intend to dissolve the Treaty of 1815 for good cause."

The grand duke cleared his throat. "As far as I'm concerned, it's history. No pun intended."

The two men laughed.

A weight lifted from Jack's soul. He was free—and

only by being free could he convince Kim that he truly loved her.

Until now, he hadn't been able to separate himself from his duty. Schooled since boyhood to become a prince, Jack had not hesitated when he found himself required to fly to America and offer marriage to a stranger.

But since he'd met Kim, Jack's view of the world had changed so completely that he no longer fit the role he had been tailored for. He still placed his country's well-being above his own, but he placed Kim's there, too.

The future rested in her hands. He only hoped that during their time together the same feelings had transformed them both.

"Where's Angela?" asked Kristoffer. "I hope she'll forgive me for bringing that woman."

"She went back to the palace with Kim." Jack decided there was no point in mentioning his plans to marry Angela, since it would no longer be necessary.

The grand duke's expression darkened. "Who's with them?"

"Pierre's driving, and there's a guard."

"Well, it pays to be cautious." The diver sat up, stifling a groan as he jostled his leg. "I gathered from what I heard in my father's court that there's some kind of inside contact. He may become a threat, now that everything else has failed."

Jack's throat tightened. He'd been careful not to reveal all his plans even to his personal staff, but in his haste to get Kim to safety he'd forgotten that a traitor might be waiting at the palace to finish the job.

"I'd better get home." He caught the other man's understanding nod. "As long as Pierre's with her, she'll be safe enough but—"

He stopped, fear pumping through him as a small discrepancy thrust itself into his consciousness.

Why had Pierre not wanted Angela to ride with them? It went completely against the man's character to suggest that the woman he adored stay behind to comfort Kristoffer.

At the time Jack had subconsciously assumed that Pierre, like him, was trying to keep the two women separated for Lindelor's sake. But Pierre didn't know that Angela could still have children. He had no reason to suggest she stay behind....

Unless he was planning to do something he shouldn't en route to the palace.

"What?" Kristoffer demanded, seeing his thunderstruck impression. "You think it's Pierre?"

"The Austrian diver," Jack said. "He stopped them yesterday before we were attacked. He knew Pierre."

"I'll come with you." The other man tried to swing his legs off the gurney, then cursed as his body refused to cooperate.

"You'd only slow me down." Jack headed for the door, shouting for Hans and the guards. Within seconds he had alerted his security forces, but he refused to rely on them. He had to save Kim himself.

Sprinting out the side exit Jack grabbed the keys from a startled soldier and revved the motorcycle to life. He prayed that Angela's presence would delay Pierre at least a little.

It was the only hope he had.

"YOU CAN'T DO THIS," Angela said.

The limousine lurched and bumped as it headed along an unpaved trail. "It's very sad," Pierre told them from the front seat. "Our guard turns out to be a crazed terrorist from, oh, pick any country. Except Zakovia, of course. He forces us into the mountains and across the border, kills the princess, knocks me out and—what about you, Angela? You could escape with a few cuts and bruises, you know.''

Through her window, Kim studied the motorcyclist riding alongside, an acne-scarred man with broad cheekbones. From his harsh expression, she could expect no leeway there.

Her mind raced through the possibilities. Jumping from the car would accomplish nothing, even if it were possible to get the door open, which she doubted. Her pepper spray had been used up and she had no other weapon. Neither did Angela, who hadn't even brought a purse.

But Jack had tucked a gun beneath the back seat. He'd shown it to her before they left the palace this morning.

''I'm not a traitor!'' Angela flared.

''You'll change your mind in a few minutes,'' Pierre said. ''What's the point of dying for nothing, when you could marry a man who loves you?''

The gun was beneath Angela's seat. Visually, Kim measured the distance and realized that somehow she would have to alert the other woman or change places, without arousing Kristoffer's suspicion.

''A villain who tried to kill me by greasing the pavement?'' Angela demanded.

The blond man grimaced. ''I didn't learn of it until afterward. I would have prevented it if I could. But it did save you from marrying Prince Jack.''

''Don't kid yourself.'' Angela tried a door handle, but as Kim had anticipated it refused to budge. ''Hell will freeze before I consent to marry *you!*''

''Don't be so sure.'' Turning, the aide gave them

an easy smile. "Zakovia has an old law allowing the prince to command a marriage, whether the woman wills it or not. By tonight you'll be my wife, Angela. We can even have the document backdated. Then, if you open your mouth, we'll make you look like a traitor who's trying to play both sides."

Kim only half listened as she focused on retrieving the weapon. Could she pretend to faint? Falling on the floor might put her within grabbing distance. On the other hand, Angela would almost certainly lean over to check on her, making it impossible to get off a shot at Pierre.

"I don't understand," the young woman said. "Why are you doing this?"

The car jounced around a pothole. "I'm tired of being nobody. How far can I rise in this kingdom of happy sheep? Prince Igor has promised to make me governor of Lindelor. It will be my palace then. And yours, too, if you like."

Kim had run out of ideas for anything remotely subtle. Instead, she pointed out Angela's window and shouted, "What's that?"

The other woman and Pierre both turned to look. Kim dived for the floor and came up with the gun.

Alarm flashed across the secretary's face. Something whirred and Kim realized a partition was closing between the front and back seat, clear panels zooming toward each other from both sides. Desperately, she pulled the trigger, but the gun only clicked.

"You forgot to take the safety off." Pierre's voice hummed over an intercom. "And fortunately for me the partition is bulletproof. Try that again and you're more likely to shoot yourself with a ricochet than to harm me."

Kim sucked in a shaky breath. "At least it's a standoff. You won't be able to get at us."

"Oh?" The driver's mouth twisted mockingly. "Did I forget to mention *how* our terrorist friend was going to kill you? He's wired the car with a bomb. I'll be thrown clear, and so will Angela, if she agrees. I presume you wouldn't shoot her to keep her from escaping, would you, Your Highness?"

Of course she wouldn't hurt Angela, Kim thought as she clutched the gun. But once the door opened to let Angela out, she might get a chance at one of the men.

In a low voice the other woman said, "Do you know how to take the safety off?"

Kim shook her head. "I've never fired one of these," she admitted in a whisper.

"I have," Angela murmured back. "I was in the reserves for two years. If you don't mind—?"

For an instant, suspicion flashed through Kim's mind. Was it possible the other woman might be in league with the Zakovians and trying to disarm her?

She dismissed the thought. These past weeks Angela had shown she wanted neither Jack's power nor his money. What she wanted was Kristoffer, a man so decent he had risked his life today to save Kim's.

Below Pierre's line of sight, she slid the gun to Angela. She just hoped the other woman would have the sense to avoid revealing that she was capable of bearing children.

One of them had to live and save Lindelor. The people couldn't be consigned to misery under a tyrant like Igor.

But Angela, clutching the gun beneath a fold of her skirt, seemed energized by new bravado. "You're an idiot to think this will work, Pierre."

"Because you love the grand duke? He'll be disinherited," the driver growled over the intercom. "Prince Jack has cast you aside. I'm the only one who can give you a palace now."

"Be quiet," Kim murmured, touching Angela's arm, but the other woman shook her off.

"Jack never cast me aside!" Angela blurted. "I lied to him. I—" She stopped at last, catching the horror behind Kim's fierce gaze. "I mean, uh—"

They hit a rock, bouncing so hard Kim nearly lost her balance, but Pierre barely flinched. "You lied to him? You can still have children?"

From Angela's stunned silence, Kim knew she recognized how much more desperate their situation had just become.

The door would never open, there would be no chance to shoot the men and the car would explode with both of them inside.

IT TOOK LONG, agonizing minutes to learn from the posted guards where the limousine had turned off the main roads and headed into the countryside. Was Pierre taking the women to Zakovia? If so, Jack had no doubt that somewhere along the way he would kill Kim.

As he roared off the main track onto a rocky byway, the Lindelorian soldiers and police officers strung out behind. Caution slowed their progress as they struggled to avoid potholes and rocks.

But Jack knew no fear, except that of losing Kim. With every ounce of his athletic training, he flung his bike forward.

Over ruts and cracks he rocketed, careening from side to side to avoid the worst obstacles. Once a loose scatter of gravel sent him into a skid, but Jack pulled out of it with a desperate surge of power.

At first glance, the countryside appeared open, but clumps of trees and a gradual rise made it impossible to see far ahead. Had he taken the wrong route? Had Pierre given him the slip?

Silently, Jack cursed his own lack of preparation. He'd imagined that he had foreseen everything, but the Zakovians had been ahead of him at every turn.

He'd been so damn confident that everything was under control. And all the time Pierre had been a turncoat, right under his nose.

Ahead, the trail veered around a boulder and rose steeply toward the mountains. The border with Zakovia lay only about a mile farther.

To cross it with an armed guard would constitute an act of war. Well, so was kidnapping a princess.

But as Jack swept past the boulder, he saw that crossing the border was no longer an issue. The white limousine rumbled up the path less than a thousand feet ahead.

Alongside it rode a cyclist wearing heavy protective gear. As Jack gunned his engine, the man spun to a halt. Sunlight gleamed off a submachine gun on the back of the cycle.

Before the guard could swing it into position, Jack whipped around him, expecting at any minute to hear bullets whistling past. They didn't come. Perhaps the man had remembered that if a Zakovian agent killed the prince, the treaty would be null and void. Or maybe he simply hadn't been ready in time.

But the echo of automated fire behind told him the man had no compunctions when it came to stopping the security forces. Jack was alone.

He could see the limousine slowing above him as

the path narrowed. How did Pierre expect to take a limousine along a mountain trail barely adequate for off-road vehicles?

With a growing sense of dread, Jack twisted the accelerator bar and the motorcycle zoomed forward, bucking on the steep path. Why was Pierre halting? And why was he opening his door, when he would be safer behind its bulletproof protection?

Jack's alarm intensified as the blond man leaped out and darted away, shouting at the gun-wielding guard below to hurry up. For a frozen instant the prince was torn between his urge to tackle the traitor and his instinct to make sure Kim was all right.

Then a pounding from inside the car drew his gaze to the women's faces visible through the rear windshield. They were beating on it and shouting.

He saw the shape of the word rather than heard it. *Bomb! Bomb!*

Jack ditched his cycle alongside the limo. After a futile attempt to wrench open the rear doors, he flung himself into the front seat that Pierre had just vacated.

Above the noise of the engine, he heard an ominous clicking. It came from somewhere below, possibly the chassis.

There was no time to find and disable the device, even if he had possessed the knowledge and tools to do so. His only hope was to free the women.

When the transparent partition failed to yield to several strong blows, Jack transferred his attention to the instrument panel. Frantically, he pushed one button after another.

The front windows went down, but not the rear ones. The trunk popped open, but the back doors stayed locked. Someone had redesigned this car to make it especially difficult to deactivate the trap.

"Can you hear me?" he yelled.

"Yes!" came the women's voices over a speaker.

"There must be a panic button in the back. The guy who owns this thing wouldn't build it so he could be locked in. Find it!"

As he searched under the dash for a hidden lever, he could hear the women scrambling behind. Outside, a motorcycle roared toward them and Pierre shouted, "Over here! Step on it!"

"I found it!" came Kim's voice, followed an instant later by a gasp of dismay. "It doesn't work! They must have disconnected it."

"Oh, rot!" added Angela. "Pierre's getting away!"

Jack didn't care about Pierre. He only cared about finding a release for the rear doors. It had to be here somewhere, right in front of him, somewhere obvious.

"Jack!" Kim yelled. "Get out of the car! There's no reason for you to die too!"

Then he saw it. Attached to the steering column was an arm that held the windshield-wiper controls. There were three knobs, one for the front, one for the back, and one unmarked.

Jack gave it a twist. Over the hum of the engine and the whirring of the bomb, he heard the rear locks pop open.

Flinging himself from the car, he reached the back just as Kim kicked open her door. There was no time for gentleness. With all his strength, Jack yanked her out and shoved her away, then turned to help Angela.

His cousin had already bailed out the other side and was running up the trail, shooting wildly at the escaping cycle with its two passengers. Then, from behind them, another bike flashed by in pursuit and Angela held her fire.

Pushing Kim ahead, Jack lunged away from the

limo. He felt the blast a split second before the noise reached him, and then the shock wave smashed them both to the ground.

IN THE MOMENT WHEN Jack fell atop her, shielding her from the explosion, Kim thought for a moment that her heart would stop beating.

But the only thing that mattered was whether Jack was alive. During those moments when he'd struggled to open the doors, she had been terrified that he would be killed, too.

Now, still stunned by the impact, she felt him move. As the pressure lifted, breath rasped into her lungs, along with a wave of relief.

"Kim?" It was the prince's voice, ragged with fear. "Are you hurt?"

"I don't think so. Are you?" With a shudder, she sat up. Jack sprawled on the ground beside her, sooty and bleeding from several scrapes. Beyond, she could see flames licking the blackened hulk of the car.

"I seem to be in one piece." He coughed. "Kind of a battered piece, though." He reached to wipe a smudge from her cheek. "Did I ever tell you that you're beautiful when you're dirty?"

Kim didn't know whether to laugh or cry. Instead of doing either, she nestled against her husband as he gathered her against him. The strength of his arms and the gentleness of his lips on hers soothed away her tension.

Angela's triumphant shout drew their attention. "He got them! Hans shot out the tire!"

Motorcycles roared up the path, a whole flotilla of them. Soldiers in Lindelorian uniforms leaped down to help the prince and princess, while others sped after the assassins.

"About time they got here," murmured Kim.

"Be careful!" Jack was calling. "They've got a submachine gun."

"Not any longer." Angela loped down the trail, unfazed. "When the tire blew, they crashed into a ravine. The weapon went flying into the shrubbery. And do you know the best part? I think I winged Pierre!"

The next few minutes passed in a blur of activity. By the time the flames in the car were extinguished, the soldiers had captured Pierre and the other assassin. Both men sported fresh bruises, and blood was seeping from a gunshot wound in Pierre's arm.

Seated on a log, Kim watched as the blond secretary stumbled forward and halted before the prince. The two men stared at each other for a long moment.

In profile, she could read disgust on Jack's face. Pierre's lips twisted into a snarl and then he looked away.

"I thought you would want to know," Jack said, "that Kristoffer has agreed to ask for Igor's abdication and to dissolve the treaty. Even if you'd succeeded, it would have accomplished nothing."

"It would have ruined your life," spat out the blond man. "That's worth something, I guess."

As a soldier propelled him away, Kim realized she had never seen such naked evil before. Even cold-blooded killers such as Gretchen and the red-haired man didn't take pleasure in trying to destroy someone who trusted them.

"It's amazing that we were both so taken in by him," observed Hans, brushing twigs off his pants as he walked up. Despite the headlong chase, his uniform was barely rumpled.

"Kris truly consented to end the treaty?" asked Angela. "How is his leg, by the way?"

"Broken." Jack's mouth curved in a wry grin. "Along with his heart. You'd better get back to the swim stadium and cheer him up."

"I'd suggest we all get back." Hans, as usual, put duty first. "The people are waiting for the closing ceremonies, and I'm sure they're very anxious about Your Highnesses."

"My wife has been through a lot. Under the circumstances, I don't think she should be expected to make a public appearance," Jack said.

Kim shook her head. "I want everyone to see that I'm okay."

Jack regarded her dubiously and then he smiled. "My princess with nerves of steel. Well, come along then." He took her arm, helping maintain her shaky balance over the uneven trail as they headed for a police car.

"What about—" Kim winced as she jolted her knee on a rough spot. She hadn't realized it until now, but her body was a mass of bruises. "What about your announcement?"

"The treaty's going to be dissolved," Angela pointed out. "All bets are off."

"What announcement?" said Hans.

"I'll tell you on the way," said the prince.

Chapter Sixteen

As it turned out, the police car wasn't large enough to seat the four of them comfortably, so Angela went in a second one with Hans. Presumably she would explain on the way about her restored fertility.

Leaning against her husband's shoulder as an officer piloted their car back to the swim center, Kim soaked up Jack's nearness. The chase had left him with a faint tang from his exertion that blended tantalizingly with his usual piney scent.

From this position, she could feel the rapid beating of his heart and the deep intake of his breath. Even though he no longer needed to assure the succession, he had risked his life to save her. And Angela, too, of course. Whatever the future might hold, she felt an abiding admiration for Jack's courage and goodness.

But she had no claim on him. It wasn't just a matter of having given him permission to dissolve their marriage. Matters went much deeper than that, to the core of their relationship.

The prince had come to her in the first place out of duty. Although he had tricked her by withholding the truth about the million dollars after she suffered amnesia, he had never pretended that he was marrying for love.

Kim had known from the beginning that her options were to produce an heir or to withdraw from the arrangement. There had never been any other possibility.

Certainly Jack was not obligated to remain married to her now that their union served no patriotic purpose. And didn't he have the right to choose his own wife, as any other man would?

She had made love to him of her own free will. No matter what happened, she would never regret that decision. The special moments between them would remain fresh in her mind until the day she died.

Studying her husband, she saw that he was gazing at the streets through which they drove with an intensity that bespoke his love for his country. There was an air of sadness in his expression—perhaps, she thought, at how close he had come to losing everything to Zakovia.

With a start, Kim realized that she loved this place, too. She loved the way the shopkeepers waved at their prince and the way he smiled back. She loved the flowers brightening in each window box and patch of garden.

She loved the crisp air and the mountains towering overhead and Aunt Rapunzel's bravery and Lady Nanette's refusal to gossip. She loved Angela's forthrightness, and the finicky way Hans had brushed twigs off his uniform as if wild deeds of derring-do were no excuse for untidiness.

A tight knot of pain formed in her chest at the knowledge that she would soon be leaving this place. There was no point in pretending that she wanted to go back to her old life.

But she owed Jack the same fairness he had shown toward her. She would not renege on her word. Just as Lindelor had been liberated from the threat of Zakovian dominance, Jack should be liberated to marry as he pleased.

Outside the swimming stadium citizens of Lindelor in traditional garb and tourists draped with cameras formed a sea of humanity, standing quietly and watching the road. A moment after Kim saw them, Jack leaned from his window and the onlookers responded with a huge cheer, a spontaneous cry of joy and relief.

When the police car pulled to the curb and a guard opened the door, no one pressed in or grabbed at them. Instead the people cleared a path to the entrance, their faces bright with happiness. A few called their good wishes, but otherwise there was a remarkable lack of noise or disorder.

Kim was surprised to hear her name arise from the crowd. "Princess Kimberly is safe! Long live Princess Kim!"

Startled, she followed Jack's example by waving and then accompanied him inside. She hoped the citizens would understand, when they learned that she was leaving, that it wasn't because she didn't love them.

Inside, at Hans's insistence, she and Jack and Angela stopped by the clinic to make sure there were no undetected internal injuries. The main damage, in Kim's opinion, was to her skirt, which had to be safety pinned at the hem, along with some dirt smears that she damp-wiped from Jack's coat.

Kristoffer, whose leg cast already boasted a half-dozen signatures, reached for Angela's hand as soon as she came in. From their beaming faces, Kim could see they would be having their own private reconciliation later.

Hans vanished for a while and then returned, his thin features alight with glee. "Your Highness," he said, making a low bow, "I regret to inform you that I am resigning my position as foreign minister."

"You don't look very regretful," Jack said as the doctor applied antiseptic to his facial cuts.

"And I humbly request to be assigned to the Lindelorian trade mission in Los Angeles," Hans continued. "I recommend Ladislaw Munchen as my replacement here."

"Congratulations," said the prince.

"Your Highness accepts my proposal?" asked Hans.

"The congratulations are on your engagement to Miss Valerie Norris. I presume that's why you're moving to Los Angeles." Jack clapped his old friend on the back. "Good for you."

At least she would still have one friend from Lindelor when she got home, Kim reflected. "That's wonderful! We'll enjoy welcoming you into the family!"

"Indeed!" was all Hans managed to say.

As the doctor checked Kim's bruised knee to make sure it needed no further treatment, she saw the same regretful expression on Jack's face that she had noticed as they passed through the town. Despite his happiness for Hans, he must be anticipating how he would miss his closest adviser.

At last they received a clean bill of health. After a brief delay while the women made emergency repairs to their grooming and a wheelchair was provided for Kristoffer, the small group emerged to formally close the Prince's Cup.

The competitors stood around the outdoor pool, each team wearing its own colors. Medals gleamed in the sunshine. It was too bad, Kim thought, that the grand duke had been forced to sacrifice his chance at one, but he didn't seem to mind.

Onlookers packed the stands, including many people Kim had come to know at the palace. Minicams bearing the logo of TV Lindelor swept the scene.

An anchorman whom Kim recognized from earlier broadcasts approached, holding out a microphone. "We're broadcasting live, Your Highness," the man told the prince. "The news has swept Europe about the princess's kidnapping."

"I'm happy to say that she's safe and so is my cousin, Angela," Jack responded for the viewing audience. "In just a moment, Grand Duke Kristoffer of Zakovia will have a statement to make, and then so will I."

Kim stifled a shudder. She would need to appear unruffled as Jack announced their pending divorce. It would be unfair to him if she showed any sign of her anguish.

A deal was a deal, whether in business or in politics. And that, she reminded herself, was what this marriage was about: politics, not love.

Because Kristoffer's wheelchair made it impractical to reach the top of the stands, a platform with a ramp had been hastily erected at one side. Nearby, Kim spotted a group of excited children holding cages of doves, which would be released to mark the end of the competition.

The birds were a symbol of liberty, something she had long cherished. Today, though, freedom seemed like a heavy responsibility.

Seats had been provided on the platform for the two women. Mindful of the need to uphold Lindelorian dignity, Kim slid into place with a smoothness that would have astonished anyone who knew her old self. Angela plopped down beside her, too chipper to worry about being graceful.

As the onlookers leaned forward expectantly, the minicams took aim. Stepping forward, Jack spoke into the microphone.

"First, I want to assure you that Princess Kimberly and my cousin, Angela Schnappsenfeld, are unharmed despite an assassination attempt. The kidnappers have been captured and will face trial. One of them, I regret to say, was killed. I extend my condolences to her family."

From where she sat behind him, Kim noted that his shoulders were straight and proud beneath the scarlet jacket, giving no sign of the soreness that must be setting in by now. In the days to come, she thought, he would surely enjoy soaking in the hot spring-fed pool at the palace.

She could almost feel its heat and smell its faintly sulfurous odor. Her aunt's hot tub would be a poor substitute. Kim only hoped this knife-edged yearning to be with Jack would fade along with her bruises.

"As you can see, Grand Duke Kristoffer of Zakovia suffered a broken leg saving my wife. I'm pleased to report that he is expected to make a full recovery," the prince continued. "Now he has a few words to say."

Polite applause sounded as Jack adjusted the microphone's height and turned it over to Kristoffer. Although she could see only a little of his face, Kim noted that the grand duke had grown uncharacteristically solemn.

"A terrible wrong has been attempted today by my father, Prince Igor," Kristoffer said. "He has sent assassins—and not for the first time—to try to kill Princess Kimberly."

A gasp went up at this open admission that the Zakovian ruler was behind the attack.

"An attempt was also made on the life of Lady Angela, the woman I intend to marry," Kristoffer continued. "My father did these things because he wants to rule Lindelor. He needs this country's resources because he has bankrupted Zakovia with his reckless spending and inept government."

Beside Kim, Angela leaned close. "He's certainly not pulling any punches."

Kim didn't dare respond, not when the cameras were broadcasting this event all over Europe. She suspected that, adjusting for the time difference, at least a few clips would show up on American networks as well.

Whatever notoriety resulted would quickly die, she hoped. At best it might net her a few new real-estate clients impressed at meeting a former princess.

"I therefore call upon the people of Zakovia to rise up and throw off the yoke of Prince Igor." Kristoffer spread his arms in a grand gesture. "To the captain of the palace guard and the commanding general of the army, I urge you to join with me and remove him peacefully. I promise you will be treated with honor and considered for positions on my staff."

The Zakovian swim team shifted uneasily, but the people of Lindelor responded with loud cheers.

"And finally," Kristoffer said, "my first act as prince of Zakovia will be to dissolve the Treaty of 1815, which gave us the right to take over Lindelor if the royal line of succession came to an end. Let our nations no longer be predator and prey, but friends and allies from now on."

To tumultuous applause, the grand duke shook hands with the prince. Then the two men raised their arms together, hands clasped in a victory salute.

At last it was the Lindelorian ruler's turn to speak. As he took the microphone, Kim's heart thrummed painfully. Sweat dampened her hands, and she buried them in her skirt.

"Now I come to a much more personal matter, one that is painful to me," Jack told the hushed audience.

The sound of her own heartbeat roared in Kim's ears. She could hardly bear to listen. Only a resolve not to embarrass Jack kept her rooted in her seat.

"As soon as Lindelor is freed from the Treaty of 1815, my first act will be to abdicate my throne," said the prince.

In the shocked moment that followed, Kim stared at the man's crimson-coated back. What on earth was he planning? She had expected him to take advantage of his new freedom, but nothing as extreme as this.

"The people of Lindelor will be free to choose a new ruler or to adopt a democratic form of government," Jack said.

Beside him, Kristoffer shook his head in amazement. The expression on Hans's face was nothing short of thunderstruck.

"Your Highness!" said the foreign minister. "No one wishes you to do such a thing."

A murmur of agreement rose from the watchers, but the prince lifted his hand for silence. "I wish it," he said, and half turned toward Kim. "You see, I have done something I ought not to have done. I've fallen in love. My wife, who married me only to assure the Lindelorian succession, generously agreed to come here and risk her life to help catch the Zakovian assassins. But it is time for her to return home, and I can only hope that she will allow me to go with her."

Kim's mouth dropped open but no words came out. Jack was abdicating because of her?

"Your Highness?" Hans was speaking to Kim, not to Jack, she realized. "Can't you make him see reason?"

Before she could respond, the prince knelt on the platform. Alpine sunshine highlighted the strong planes of his face as he spoke. "I will continue to serve my country as a goodwill ambassador, but first I must ask Princess Kimberly if she will allow me to come with her and be her true husband, for I will love her until I die."

Tears welled in Kim's eyes. A part of her registered that hundreds—perhaps millions—of people were waiting for her answer. But she saw only Jack. It was hard to believe that this sophisticated, powerful man had fallen in love with her so completely. Somewhere during those moments of laughter and danger, in the transition from mutual suspicion to shared passion, he had changed just as she had.

She knew how much he loved his country and how well he served as its ruler. He didn't really want to leave, and neither did she.

An elbow in her side jostled Kim from her reverie as Angela hissed, "Go to it! Put the chap out of his misery!"

For a moment Kim didn't know how to proceed. With no experience in making public appearances, she felt acutely conscious of the cameras and the onlookers.

Then she gazed into Jack's deep green eyes, mirrors of her own, and forgot about the world.

Somehow she managed to rise and stand facing the kneeling prince. *You silly goose, I love you too,* didn't seem like quite the thing to say under the circumstances, and for a moment she feared the right words wouldn't come.

Leaning over, Hans murmured, "How about starting with, 'Don't be an idiot.'"

"I heard that," Jack responded, loudly enough for the microphone to pick up. "My minister is coaching you. No fair."

"It's perfectly fair, since he's about to marry my aunt and become my uncle," Kim replied. "Herr Frick is the one who's moving to Los Angeles, but you're staying right here, Your Highness."

His jaw tightening, Jack got to his feet. "Is that your final answer?"

"Well, I certainly hope you're staying here," said Kim, "because I am."

For a long moment, he stared as if uncertain of her meaning. Then the grim line of his mouth softened. "You would stay here with me?"

"I love you, too," she said.

Happiness glowed in his face as he lifted her hand and brushed his lips across it. "Forever and always?"

"Forever and always," whispered Kim.

In the stands, a flurry of handkerchiefs marked the response as onlookers wiped their eyes and sniffled. "Your Highness!" prompted Hans under his breath. "Would you please unabdicate before we suffer a governmental crisis?"

"I withdraw my plans to abdicate," said Jack, "on the provision that Princess Kimberly will rule alongside me."

"Done," she said.

Applause rippled from the stands, swelling into a

thunder of approval. Even the Zakovian team was cheering, and on someone's signal the children near the stage opened their cages and the air filled with the beating wings of doves.

Forever and always, thought Kim. That sounded like long enough to be with Jack, almost.

LOVE *or* MONEY?
Why not Love *and* Money!
After all, millionaires
need love, too!

How to Marry a
MILLIONAIRE

Suzanne Forster,
Muriel Jensen
and
Judith Arnold

bring you three original stories
about finding that one-in-a million man!

Harlequin also brings you
a million-dollar sweepstakes—enter
for your chance to win a fortune!

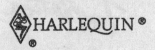

HARLEQUIN ®

It's hot...and it's out of control!

Beginning this spring, Temptation turns up the *heat*. Look for these bold, provocative, *ultra*sexy books!

#629 OUTRAGEOUS
by Lori Foster (April 1997)

#639 RESTLESS NIGHTS
by Tiffany White (June 1997)

#649 NIGHT RHYTHMS
by Elda Minger (Sept. 1997)

BLAZE: Red-hot reads—only from

Everyone loves the *Holidays*...

Four sexy guys with two things in common:
the Holiday name and humbug in the heart!

PETER

the holiday heart

MICHAEL

by Linda Cajio

This year Cupid and his romantic cohorts are
working double—make that quadruple—time, not only
Valentine's Day but also Mother's Day, Labor Day and
Christmas—every holiday season throughout 1997.

Don't miss any of these heartfelt romances in:

May—#678 BACHELOR DADDY

September—#694 BOSS MAN

November—#704 MISTER CHRISTMAS

JARED

RAYMOND

Only from Harlequin American Romance.

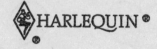